PADDLE BATTLE

Eric Howling

PADDLE BATTLE

Eric Howling

James Lorimer & Company Ltd., Publishers
Toronto

James Lorimer & Company Ltd., Publishers acknowledges funding support from
the Ontario Arts Council (OAC), an agency of the Government of Ontario.
We acknowledge the support of the Canada Council for the Arts, which
last year invested $153 million to bring the arts to Canadians throughout the
country. This project has been made possible in part by the Government of
Canada and with the support of Ontario Creates.

Cover design: Tyler Cleroux
Cover image: iStock

Library and Archives Canada Cataloguing in Publication (Paperback)

Title: Paddle battle / Eric Howling.
Names: Howling, Eric, 1956- author.
Series: Sports stories.
Description: Series statement: Sports stories
Identifiers: Canadiana (print) 20210202351 | Canadiana (ebook) 20210202386
    | ISBN 9781459416239 (softcover) | ISBN 9781459416246 (EPUB)
Classification: LCC PS8615.O9485 P33 2021 | DDC jC813/.6—dc23

Published by: Distributed in Canada by: Distributed in the US by:
James Lorimer &   Formac Lorimer Books   Lerner Publisher Services
Company Ltd., Publishers   5502 Atlantic Street   241 1st Ave. N.
117 Peter Street, Suite 304   Halifax, NS, Canada   Minneapolis, MN, USA
Toronto, ON, Canada   B3H 1G4   55401
M5V 0M3   www.lernerbooks.com
www.lorimer.ca

Printed and bound in Canada.
Manufactured by Friesens Corporation in Altona, Manitoba,
Canada in June 2021.
Job #277238

For Cooper, my favourite paddler.

Contents

1 Race FACE

"Let's go, Finn!" Niko shouted.

He sat in the cockpit just ahead of me. His strong arms pulled the blades of his paddle through the churning water beside our kayak.

We were racing against two other boats from our Okanagan Kayak Club. Chad and Sanjay were blasting their sprint kayak through the course in the lane to our left. Leo and Theo's sleek boat was flying on our right. We were all gunning for a spot on the U15 squad for the national championships in Ottawa. No one wanted to lose. We all wanted Coach Cooper to pick us for the team going to Ontario in August.

Niko and I had started the race strong. Our blades hit the water at exactly the same moment. Every time Niko took a stroke on the left side, I matched him with one of my own. Every time he dug in his paddle on the right, I did the same. We were in perfect sync. Our kayak was a red torpedo shooting straight through the deep blue waters of Lake Okanagan.

Paddle Battle

For the first 200 metres of the race we were in the lead. Stroke . . . stroke . . . stroke, we took off like a bullet. I shot glances to both sides and didn't see the other two boats. I smiled. *No one is going to catch us today*, I thought. But the race was a thousand metres long. There was still a lot of paddling ahead of us.

We kept up the pressure on the other two kayaks. With every stroke, our rounded blades scooped the water alongside our hull. Spray kicked up against our hands and arms, but we gripped the shafts of our paddles tight. We couldn't let go. A slip could cause even a single missed stroke, and that could spell defeat. Over and over, we pulled our black blades through the water. We knew that, with each stroke, we were getting closer to the finish line.

From the corner of my eye I spotted the pointed tip of a blue boat in the left lane. Chad and Sanjay! My eyes darted to the right lane and saw a green tip. Leo and Theo! *How could this be happening?* I wondered. Both the other kayaks were catching up. All three boats were neck and neck and neck, rocketing between the white buoys marking the course. Anyone could win.

Niko put his head down. His black hair was wet with sweat. "Come on, Finn!" he shouted.

I kept driving my blades into the water, trying to match Niko's frantic pace. My arms burned. My back ached as we pushed forward. But something was wrong. No matter how hard we paddled, the teams in the other two lanes were pulling ahead. They were leaving us in their wakes.

There was no way I was the problem. The year before, I had been one of the best U15 paddlers in the province. Not bad for a thirteen year old. I even had a gold trophy in my bedroom to prove it. This year my results hadn't been as good. But how bad could I really be? Maybe I wasn't training as much as before, but I had my reasons. No, the problem was definitely Niko. He was the one slowing us down.

"Bring it!" Niko shouted, paddling even faster.

I pulled my blades through the swirling water as hard as I could, but I couldn't keep up. Part of me didn't want to keep up.

Now our strokes were out of sync. The tips of our blades started to hit each other. Our narrow boat started to rock. Sprint kayaks are built for speed, not for lurching back and forth like a seesaw. Spray started to wash over the sides into our boat.

Chad and Sanjay crossed the finish line far ahead of us. They whooped as they raised their paddles in victory. Leo and Theo powered across a couple of seconds later for second place. All four paddlers turned their heads to see where the third-place kayak was. They all wanted to know what had happened to the boat that was supposed to win.

Niko and I dipped our blades into the water one last time and struggled across the finish line. Our kayak was heavy with water. Three inches of Lake Okanagan sloshed around in the bottom.

Slumped over and gasping for breath, Niko was so tired he couldn't speak. Our kayak glided for a few seconds before he whipped around to face me. His eyes were filled with anger. "What was that, man?" he snapped.

"We took on water." I nodded at the liquid swishing around the bottom of our boat.

"No kidding!" Niko shot back. "It's like we were paddling in a bathtub." He splashed a handful of lake water out of the kayak in disgust. "I'm in front. I set the stroke rate. It's your job to keep up with me, Finn."

"You were paddling too fast," I said. I knew it was just an excuse.

"That's because we were losing." Niko narrowed his eyes at me. "We still had a chance to win."

"I didn't think we did." I shrugged. "We were in last place. It was all over."

"It's like you gave up. Like you just didn't care." Niko shook his head at me. "That's not the way you used to be, Finn."

"Well, that's the way I am now." I turned my head away, not wanting to meet Niko's glare.

"I want to make the team going to nationals," Niko said through clenched teeth. "But I don't know if I can with you as my partner. You're always letting me down."

I knew Niko was counting on me. It was a two-man kayak, after all. We both had to do our part. The only problem was that Niko wanted it more than I did.

"Making the nationals is no big deal," I said blankly.

"It is to me," Niko snarled. "I want to be on the team. I don't want to be left behind."

I slammed my blade into the water. The kayak slowed to a stop. "You don't know anything about being left behind," I said bitterly.

We paddled back to the dock in silence. A grey haze was hanging in the distance. It was a reminder of the wildfires that were burning farther north. I took a deep breath. The faint smell of smoke filled the air.

"Good effort, everyone," Coach Cooper said. He stood above us on the dock. When I looked up at him, his shoulders were so broad they blocked out the sun. "But I'll be expecting more from you guys when school's out for the summer. That includes you, Finn." Coach stared down at Niko and me, still floating in our kayak. "If you and Niko want to make it to nationals, you're going to have to work together as a team. I know you can do better."

After Niko got out, I stayed sitting in the kayak a while longer. I wondered if Coach and Niko were right. If I did just quit trying. If maybe it was my fault we came last. If I even wanted to do better. I wasn't sure. All I knew was that everything had changed since Mom left.

2 Making the GRADE

I was surprised when Niko grabbed a desk two rows over instead of his usual one. He usually sat right behind me in our grade-eight homeroom. It seemed strange for him to choose another seat, especially since this was the very last day of school. We were just here to pick up our report cards and leave. We had been friends for years. But after what happened during our race on the weekend, I guess I should have seen it coming. He gave me a nod, but didn't say anything. I guess he was still mad at me for not winning.

Niko and I weren't the only paddlers in classroom 8B. Soon, Chad and Sanjay would also be staring at the "HAVE A GREAT SUMMER!" message that Ms. Putnam had scrawled on the whiteboard. Next door, Leo and Theo would be listening to their teacher, Mr. Martinez. We would usually all meet up at lunch and grab pizza, fries, a hot dog or some other fast food in the cafeteria. But lately I hadn't always felt like it. Sometimes I even ate by myself.

Sanjay waltzed in with a big grin plastered on his face. And why wouldn't he? Sanjay was the brain of the class. He didn't have to worry about the report cards our teacher was about to give to each of us at the front of the class. I wasn't so lucky.

Ms. Putnam scanned the classroom, eyeing her prey like a hawk. Then she called us up one at a time to deliver the news, good or bad. It was all secretly hidden in the white envelopes neatly stacked on her desk.

"Sanjay," Ms. Putnam said. Her thin lips widened into a rare smile.

Springing out of his chair, Sanjay stood and hurried to the front desk. Ms. Putnam spoke a few muffled words that the rest of us couldn't make out. We all tried to listen, but Ms. Putnam was careful to speak quietly. We knew her whispers were filled with high praise, though. All you had to do was look at the massive size of Sanjay's grin. I rolled my eyes as he clutched his prized envelope and practically skipped out of the room.

Ms. Putnam glanced around. "Niko, you're in a different seat today."

Niko wasn't as quick out of his seat as Sanjay had been. He took his time shuffling up the aisle. He didn't love school like Sanjay did, but his parents put a lot of pressure on him to do well. Sometimes during the last month, he wasn't even allowed to paddle at the club if he had a test the next day. Having his parents on his case all the time must have worked, though. He always seemed to get a lot of high marks. After his short interview with Ms. Putnam, Niko strolled out of our grade-eight door for the last time. Before leaving, he gave me a look that said, *See if you can top this, Finn.*

"Mr. Barnes." Ms. Putnam pointed a finger at Chad.

The first thing Chad always did when called on was to flick his mop of hair out of his eyes. Some people in class thought he never got a haircut, but they were wrong. He was always getting it cut, or 'styled,' as he'd say. Chad just wanted to look surfer-dude cool or something. And he could afford to get a haircut anytime he wanted. His dad had started some tech company that had been bought by Google. Now they were raking in the cash. None of us could believe his good luck.

Chad flicked his hair and swaggered to the front of the class. His smug smile told everyone it didn't matter what kind of marks he got. He would always be able to buy whatever he wanted. After a few words from Ms. Putnam, Chad was on his way to grade nine.

"Finn, did you want to come up to the front?"

Not really, I thought. I could easily wait, like maybe for the rest of the day. "Right now?"

"Yes, now would be good." Ms. Putnam smiled as best she could and patted the chair beside her. "Come have a seat."

I tilted my head, wary of her invitation. Why was I the only one that had to take a seat? Everyone else got a handshake and a ticket to freedom out the door.

"Now, Finn," Ms. Putnam began. "I know this has been a tough year for you, being without your mother and all."

I stared at her blankly. It was weird talking about my mom, especially since my teacher sort of looked like her.

"But sometimes things are darkest before the dawn," she said.

I could feel a frown wrinkling my brow. *This doesn't sound good*, I thought.

Ms. Putnam pulled the next white envelope from the pile and placed it on her desk. "You have passed every course, Finn, which is good."

Those were the words I was hoping to hear. I started to stand up, ready to make my escape.

"Not so fast." Ms. Putnam held up her hand like a stop sign. "But it's not *very* good. I truly believe you are capable of so much more." Her eyes studied my face, as if I had a bad rash.

Maybe the news wasn't as good as I thought. I slumped in my chair for the longer-than-expected visit.

"Getting all Cs and Ds is really just scraping by," Ms. Putnam said. "Is that all you want to do, Finn — just scrape by?"

I didn't care that much about my marks. But I knew that wasn't what Ms. Putnam wanted to hear. "No, ma'am," I said, shaking my head.

"I think if you did a bit more math, science and socials homework, you would see a world of difference." Ms. Putnam nodded in the hope that I would too.

"I guess." I shrugged. There wasn't that much difference between getting a C and a B. And I had no idea how getting better marks was supposed to change my life.

I met Ms. Putnam's gaze and thought I saw a glimmer of a smile. "What does your father think about your schooling?" she asked. "Does he tell you to do your homework?"

I nodded, but that wasn't the whole answer. Just because he told me to do my homework didn't mean I'd always do it. Sometimes when he thought I was studying, I was actually in my room playing games online. And my scores were getting pretty good. It wasn't very hard to dodge my dad.

"Because I could ask him to remind you next school year." Ms. Putnam looked pleased with herself. "I wouldn't mind phoning him."

"I don't think that'll be necessary." I shook my head. I wanted to put a quick stop to the idea of having my teacher call my dad. That was just gross.

"Let me know if you change your mind." Ms. Putnam smiled, showing her white teeth.

I knew I never would. "Yeah, sure." I eyed her, wondering what was going on here.

Ms. Putnam finally handed me the report card.

I grabbed the white envelope and leaped to my feet, knowing that my five minutes of torture were almost over.

"You're a smart boy with a good future ahead of you, Finn," Ms. Putnam said. "You can put this year behind you and do well in grade nine. Just remember that."

I wasn't sure I'd ever forget about this year, or that I wanted to. Without wasting another second, I bolted for the door. I didn't turn back, even as Ms. Putnam called out one last reminder. "Tell your dad I said hello."

3 Guess the GUESTS

We pulled into a parking spot in front of the restaurant. Dad turned off the ignition and the car fell silent. I had no interest in having dinner with a bunch of strangers, and I let him know it.

"Tell me again why we have to meet at a fancy restaurant," I complained.

"I want it to be special, Finn."

"They're *your* friends." I rolled my eyes. "I don't even know them."

"They're going to be your friends too." Dad turned and smiled across the front seat.

I wasn't sure I liked where this was going. "What do you mean?"

"You'll find out soon enough," he said. "Just make sure you behave yourself."

Having to get dressed up in a collared shirt and nice pants wasn't my idea of a good time. Jeans and a T-shirt were all I ever wanted to wear. I didn't feel like smiling and saying please and thank you all through dinner, either. I slammed my shoulder against the door and stepped out.

The hostess showed us to our table, and we sat down in the plush chairs. The restaurant was one of those old-fashioned steakhouses with dark wood paneling. Soft piano music played in the background. I took a sip from the glass of ice water and glanced around. There were men in expensive suits and women in fancy dresses. They were sitting at tables covered by crisp, white tablecloths. At the front door, the hostess was greeting a couple of people who had just come in.

My eyes stopped scanning the room and flashed back to the entrance. *Oh no*, I thought. *That can't be . . . yeah, it is . . . that's Ms. Putnam!* I accidentally-on-purpose dropped my napkin on the floor and dove under the table to get it. *What is she doing here? Maybe celebrating the end of the school year?*

I peeked out from under the table. There was a girl about my age standing beside her. I looked closer. Ms. Putnam's daughter was here with her! Madison was in half my classes. All the guys thought she was cute, especially Chad. He was always trying to sit beside her. She was just another girl to me, though. I stayed hidden and waited for them to be shown to their seats. My only hope was that they would be seated as far away as possible from our table.

The hostess led them from the entrance and started to zigzag through the tables. I snuck another glance.

Bad idea. My teacher and her daughter were headed straight for us! *There must be some mistake*, I thought.

The hostess arrived at our table and gave my dad a warm smile. "Your guests have arrived, Mr. Hunter. Enjoy your dinner."

"Finn," Dad said, lifting the edge of the tablecloth. "Get up and say hello to our guests."

I couldn't stay out of sight any longer. I crawled out from under the table and stood awkwardly. My face was as red as the velvet curtains. I limply waved my white napkin like a surrender flag.

"Uh, hello," I croaked.

Dad jumped up. I expected him to reach out for a handshake. I wasn't ready for what happened next. He put his arms around Ms. Putnam and gave her a kiss smack on the lips.

My eyebrows shot up in disbelief. *This must be a dream*, I thought. *Or more like a nightmare.*

Dad was beaming. "Finn, I think you know Ms. Putnam and her daughter, Madison."

No kidding! I thought. *I know exactly who they are. I just saw them last week at school.*

"Good to see you again, Finn," my teacher said, as if I was still sitting beside her desk in class. "Are you enjoying your summer vacation?"

I was until my teacher showed up at dinner and lip-locked my dad, I thought. But I knew I couldn't say that. "Yeah, it's been okay."

"Your dad has told me a lot of nice things about you." Ms. Putnam smiled politely. "I hear you're a rower."

I narrowed my eyes at Dad, then turned back to Ms. Putnam. "I'm actually a kayak paddler. Rowing is a completely different sport. A lot of people get them confused."

Ms. Putnam's hand shot up to cover her mouth. "I'm so sorry, Finn. I should have known better."

Yeah, you would have known better if my dad had explained it to you right, I thought.

"Madison is a swimmer," Dad said, as we all took our seats.

"Close," Madison said, rolling her eyes. "I'm a diver."

"I knew it had something to do with a pool," Dad said, nodding.

So far things are going great, I thought. I didn't know why my teacher was here and neither parent had any idea what sports their kids competed in.

"So you're probably wondering why we're all here together." Dad grinned at everyone around the table. "Ms. Putnam — that is, Tracy — and I have been seeing each other for a few months now. We thought it would be a good idea for everyone to meet in person."

My mouth hung open like I was a dead fish.

Ms. Putnam nodded at me. "Finn, your dad and I met at your last parent-teacher interview, and things just took off from there."

"I called Tracy up and asked her out to lunch." Dad gazed at Ms. Putnam like he was in a trance.

"And I said yes!" My teacher giggled, then reached across the table to hold my dad's hand.

I thought I was going to throw up.

It seemed like only yesterday that Mom packed her bags and walked out the door. It was the worst day of my life. The memory was stuck in my brain like a bad video that kept playing over and over again.

I didn't know what my dad was doing. For all I knew he was going to get married again and Ms. Putnam would become my stepmom. I could hardly breathe.

I glanced at Madison, who looked just as upset as I felt. She glared at her mom. Then she pushed her chair away from the table and jumped to her feet. "Does Dad know about this?" she asked accusingly.

"We're divorced now, so I can do what I want," Ms. Putnam said calmly. "I don't have to tell your father everything."

Madison's voice was as cold as ice. "I'm going to the washroom. And I'm not sure I'm coming back."

"Madison!" her mom called. "Don't be rude. Come back here right now."

There were murmurs from some of the other tables. A few heads turned our way as Madison snaked through the restaurant. She never looked back.

A waiter dressed all in black swooped in, full of

smiles. "I can see you're having a fun family gathering." His eyes panned around the table. "I hope everyone is hungry. We have some delicious dinner specials."

The waiter handed out menus and I scowled at him. This wasn't my family. And I wasn't hungry. Not even for the bun that sat on my plate.

4 Bash and THRASH

I could hear the laughter all the way from shore. Whoops and howls echoed across the calm lake. Chad, Sanjay, Theo, Leo and Niko were floating in their single kayaks, waiting for practice to start. The five boats formed a circle, and the guys had them pointing into the centre to make talking easier.

I had arrived at the club a few minutes late, so I had to hurry to catch up. From the edge of the dock, I lowered my kayak into the water and started paddling toward the group. I couldn't wait to hear the jokes my teammates were laughing at. I could use something funny.

"What great story did you want to tell us, Chad?" Sanjay asked.

I took one last stroke. My kayak glided into the circle, joining the other five boats. "I bet it's a good one," I said, eager to get in on the story.

"You're just in time, Finn," Chad said, giving me a sly look. "You'll never guess what my dad saw at a restaurant last night."

Every muscle in my body tensed. I didn't think this was a story I wanted to hear.

"Did a waiter drop a plate of spaghetti on someone?" Niko guessed.

"No, better," Chad said.

"Did someone dine and dash without paying?" Leo asked.

Chad shook his head. "Even better than that."

There were a few seconds of silence. Everyone sat in their kayaks, waiting for Chad to tell them what had happened at the restaurant.

My pulse started to race. I wanted to get out of there. I tried to paddle away, but something was stopping me.

"Where you going, Finn?" Chad said, holding the tip of my kayak. "You're going to want to hear this."

Finally, Niko couldn't wait anymore. "Tell us!"

"He saw Ms. Putnam and Finn's dad kissing." Chad's eyes grew wider with every word.

"No way!" Leo shrieked.

"Way," Chad said. "And that's not all."

"There's more?" Theo asked.

Chad scanned from face to face before speaking. "Ms. Putnam's daughter was there too."

"Madison was at dinner?" Niko asked. "She's the best-looking girl in school. Just ask Chad."

Sanjay wrinkled his brow as if he was calculating a math problem in his head. "So if Ms. Putnam was there, and Madison was there, and Finn's dad was there . . ."

Every head turned my way as Sanjay figured out the missing piece of the puzzle. "That means Finn was there too," he concluded.

The group exploded in laughter.

I clenched my jaw. "You think that's funny?" I spit out.

"Yeah, hilarious," Chad snickered. "Probably the funniest thing I've ever heard."

"So let's see," Leo said. "If your dad and Ms. Putnam get hitched that'll make Madison . . . your sister!"

Theo cracked up. "People will think you're twins, like me and Leo, because you're in the same grade."

"Maybe I'll be coming over to your house, Finn." Chad grinned. "To see Madison, not you."

"I don't know, Finn," said Niko. "Getting to spend time with a hot girl is one thing. But being her brother?"

More whoops of laughter shot across the lake.

I'd had enough. Enough of living without Mom. Enough of Dad telling me what to do. Enough of my teacher coming to dinner. Enough of my teammates laughing at me. I grabbed my paddle and shoved the side of Chad's kayak.

"What's the matter?" Chad said. "You can't take a joke, Finn?"

"Not anymore!" I pushed Chad's kayak again, this time even harder.

"Quit it!" Chad shouted. "You're going to tip me over."

"What's the matter?" I fired back. "You can't take a bit of water?"

"Yeah, I can take it," Chad said bravely. "I just don't want to get my head wet, that's all." He flicked his hair to the side.

"I don't believe you," I said, rocking his kayak. "What's the real reason, Chad?" I kept thrusting my paddle against his kayak until it was about to tip.

"Okay!" Chad yelled. "I'm not a very good swimmer."

"I didn't think so," I sneered, narrowing my eyes.

"Stop it, Finn," Niko said. "You heard him. He can't swim very well."

"I don't care," I said. "Chad should have thought of that before making fun of me." I drove the blade of my paddle hard against the side of his kayak one more time. The boat swayed to the left, then to the right. Chad dropped his paddle and held on to both sides of the kayak, trying to steady the narrow boat. But it was no use. The kayak tipped on its side and sent Chad plunging into the water.

"Now look what you've done." Sanjay paddled next to his kayaking partner so Chad could cling to his boat.

"Don't worry, he's fine," I said. I watched Chad's arms splash around in the lake. "That's why we all have to wear these life belts, just in case we fall in." Everyone checked their belts to make sure they were snug around their waists, in case they were next.

"What's going on here?" Coach Cooper shouted. No one had seen him paddling over during the bashing and thrashing.

"Finn can't take a joke," Chad said, hanging on to the edge of Sanjay's kayak. "That's what's happening, Coach."

"Do I have to remind you all that you're a team?" Coach pursed his lips and locked eyes on each one of us. "We all have to work together, to make each other better. The next time I catch any one of you making fun of someone, or dumping someone, that guy is off the team. Understood?"

Everyone nodded, including Chad. He had pulled himself back into his kayak with Sanjay's help. Chad was sopping wet, even his hair.

Coach started paddling away, his ripped arms pulling his blades smoothly through the water. "Follow me. We have a lot of work to do to get ready for nationals. Practice starts now."

5 Watchful EYE

"Looks like we've got visitors," Sanjay called out. He pointed at three small specks on the shore.

He and Chad were paddling their two-man K2 kayak ahead of Niko and me. We were on a group training session along with Leo and Theo out in the middle of the lake. It was the same kind of training we had been doing all July. For two hours we had been working hard, mixing steady paddling with bursts of high-energy sprints. It was the best way to get ready for our all-out races. Beads of sweat covered our arms and backs. Only the breeze blowing off the surrounding hills kept us cool.

I focused on the three figures watching us from the viewing deck of the boathouse. "Who do you think it is?"

"Could be the national coaches," Niko guessed. "Maybe Coach Cooper invited them to check us out before the August national championships in Ontario."

At first I didn't think that was possible. Then I

remembered Coach used to be a paddler on the Canadian Olympic team. He knew all those guys. Maybe it was the coaches from the national team, after all.

"That would be awesome!" Chad said. "I bet Coach told them about my win the other day."

"You mean our win, right, Chad?" Sanjay joked. "There are two of us in this boat, you know."

"Let's give them a show," Leo said, digging his paddle into the water. "If the national coaches want to see talent, they've come to the right place."

The race to the dock was on.

Chad and Sanjay jumped out to an early lead. Their boat cut through the rippling water like a long, thin knife. Theo and Leo were right on their tail, blades hitting the water in perfect unison. Niko and I found ourselves bringing up the rear again. But what did it matter? It wasn't a real race. The other four guys were just trying to show off.

As we paddled closer, I shot a glance at the boathouse. No question, there were three people keeping a keen eye on us. I think one even had a pair of binoculars to check out the action up close. Just like a national coach would do.

The other two boats were increasing their lead. Chad and Sanjay and Theo and Leo were all focused straight ahead. They were pumping their blades through the water as fast as they could.

Niko had laser focus too. "I don't want to be last again!" he called back to me.

As far as I was concerned, Niko was wasting his energy. *So we come third. What's the big deal?* I thought. I paddled a little harder, but I wasn't about to kill myself for some fake race.

Something flashed on shore. *What was that?* I thought. One of the spectators was waving at us. That seemed weird. Maybe one of the national coaches was just being friendly. Just trying to welcome us back to shore. I shot another glance. They weren't waving at Chad's kayak, or even at Leo's. Now all three observers were waving . . . at me.

Maybe the national coaches had come all the way from Toronto to scout me. I had made the BC team that went to nationals in Halifax last summer. They could be planning their team based on last year's performance.

I plunged my blades into the water and paddled faster to keep up with Niko. We started to fly. Soon we were even with Leo and Theo, pulling alongside them stroke for stroke.

"We can take them!" Niko shouted.

After a few more strokes, we passed them. Niko's paddle kicked up white spray as we surged ahead. Now Chad and Sanjay were in our sights. *That will impress the coaches*, I thought.

My heart pounded. My arms ached. I gripped my paddle hard and dug the blades into the water as fast as I could. There wasn't far to go. The dock was getting closer. We were almost up to Chad and Sanjay's boat.

They were fading! They couldn't take the pace. The race was ours. We were going to win!

One more stroke and I glanced again. I wanted to see the look on the coaches' faces. *"That Finn Hunter really has what it takes,"* I imagined them saying. *"He's got a real future with the national team."*

The three figures watching from the boathouse were still waving. But as we got closer, I could see that they weren't from Toronto. They weren't coaches at all. I blinked, not believing what I was seeing. Dad, Ms. Putnam and Madison were leaning over the railing of the viewing deck. They were all flapping their arms around with big grins on their faces.

I froze. My brain stopped thinking. My arms stopped pulling. Our kayak stopped charging forward.

"Nice try!" Chad shouted as he and Sanjay blasted by.

"You guys will never win," Leo jeered, cruising into second place with Theo.

Niko kept paddling. He kept pulling his blades through the water as hard as he could. He kept trying to do it himself. But it was a two-man kayak. And only one man was kayaking.

"Third place again," Niko growled, as we pulled our kayak out of the water and onto the dock. "What happened, dude? We had them."

"That happened." I pointed toward the second level of the boathouse a short distance away. Ms.

Putnam, Madison and my dad looked down at us with goofy grins.

Niko shook his head. "They don't look much like national coaches."

"Not even close," I said, lifting the back of our kayak.

Niko grabbed the front and we flipped the long, sleek craft up onto our shoulders. Then we carried it up the hill to the boathouse. The other two crews had already put their kayaks away in the long racks. Chad, Sanjay, Leo and Theo were waiting for us on the lower level. They were all staring at me with sly smiles. I knew I was in trouble.

6 Family TIME

Chad looked up at the deck where Ms. Putnam, Madison and my dad were peering down at us. "I didn't know it was family day at the kayak club," Chad snickered. "If I had known, I would have invited mine too."

"Even your new sister came." Sanjay tried to hold in a laugh, but snorted instead.

Niko was still angry at coming in last. "Finn, your paddling was so lame, I bet Ms. Putnam is here to give you a detention."

"Or maybe they came to pick you up." Leo eyed the rack where we kept our bikes. "They think it's too far for their little boy to ride home."

"You guys are all idiots!" I shouted. "If Coach finds out you're picking on me, he'll kick you off the team!"

"Really, Finn?" Chad stared me down. "And how is Coach going to find out? Are you going to rat on us, like you're a little baby?"

I was burning mad at being embarrassed. Someone

was going to pay. Chad, Sanjay, Leo, Theo and Niko were lined up like bowling pins in front of me. I put my head down and crashed through the wall of laughing teammates.

The boathouse viewing deck was on the second floor. I bolted up the stairs two at a time. Ms. Putnam, Madison and my dad were still grinning from ear to ear when I burst through the door.

"What are you guys doing here?" I shouted.

Dad's forehead wrinkled with confusion. "What do you mean, son? We thought you'd like to see us."

Ms. Putnam nodded. "Since we talked so much about Madison's diving at lunch the other day, we thought it was only fair we come to watch your kayaking."

"Well it's not fair!" I raged at my dad. "I can't have you and my teacher come watch me. What do you think my teammates are saying?"

Dad's binoculars still hung around his neck. For some reason, that made me even madder. He replied, "They're probably saying how nice it is that we're taking an interest in what you do."

"Not even close, Dad." I rolled my eyes. "They're making fun of me. Laughing at me. Making jokes. And it's all because of you guys."

I thrust my chin at Ms. Putnam. "They think you're going to be my new mother."

Ms. Putnam looked startled. "Is that what you think, Finn?"

"I don't know what I think," I fired back.

"No one can replace your mom," Ms. Putnam said, her face softening. "Not me, not anyone. She's the only mom you'll ever have. Just like no one can replace Madison's dad. But that doesn't mean your father has to be lonely for the rest of his life. Even your dad deserves to be happy."

"Does he?" I snarled. "I'm not so sure about that."

Ms. Putnam looked puzzled. "I don't see why not."

"Because he's the reason my mom left. That's why." All the anger that had been bottled up inside me poured out. "He wasn't getting along with her, so he made her leave."

Ms. Putnam drew back her head in surprise. "Is that true, Blake? Your wife left because of you?"

Dad's face went stone cold. His eyes glazed over for a few seconds like he was lost in the past. He turned to Ms. Putnam and slowly shook his head. "That's not the whole story." Then Dad locked eyes with me. "But we're trying to move on. Isn't that right, buddy?"

I hated when he called me that. Buddy was what he called me when he was trying to get me to do something I didn't want to do. Like when he hoped I'd get better marks on my report card, or that I'd mow the lawn, or that I'd forget about Mom leaving. But I wasn't about to move on. I still blamed him.

"One day she was here and the next day she wasn't," I snapped. "No more being there when I got home from school, no more dinners, no more birthdays, no more nothing. Just gone."

Dad tried to put his arm around my shoulder, but I brushed it off.

"It just seems like you're trying to replace Mom real fast." I narrowed my eyes at Dad. "It's too soon. What if she comes back? Even worse, you're trying to replace her with my teacher. And that's not all." I pointed a finger in Madison's direction. "They say she's going to be my new sister."

Madison's eyes grew wide with hurt and surprise. She took a few steps to her mother's side. Ms. Putnam put her arms up as if to protect her daughter. "I'm sorry you're so upset, Finn," she said. "That's not what we wanted. We were just trying to be like a regular family."

"Well you're not my family." I shook my head, hard. "And you never will be."

"No, it doesn't look that way, does it?" Ms. Putnam looked defeated and turned to face my dad. "We should be going, Blake."

Madison was the last to leave. The two of us were left standing alone on the deck overlooking the water.

"I'm not crazy about my mom seeing your dad either," Madison said, shaking her head.

"You're not?"

"Not at all." Madison crossed her arms. "I've a got a dad too. I don't want another one."

"So you're not trying to get them together?" I asked.

Madison rolled her eyes. "I'd do anything to keep them apart."

"Okay, so at least we agree on that." I nodded, feeling relieved we were on the same side.

Madison looked out over the water. "Just so you know, I thought your kayaking looked pretty cool, Finn." She met my eyes with a half smile. "And Chad looked like he was pretty good as well."

I chuckled. "Yeah, he's all right."

Madison started to walk away. Then she stopped and turned. "And don't worry; I'll never call you my brother."

7 SWITCH

The next morning I wanted to keep a low profile at the clubhouse. I didn't need any more razzing from my teammates. I made my way to the locker room to get changed. Chad, Sanjay, Leo, Theo and Niko were already inside putting on their singlet tops and shorts.

"Hey, look, it's Finn Putnam," Chad teased. "You all alone today, or did your teacher come with you?"

I clenched my jaw and took a step toward Chad. I was just about to tell him to get lost when the locker-room door swung open.

"What did I say about picking on each other?" Coach Cooper asked. His muscled frame filled the doorway.

"I don't know what you're talking about, Coach," Chad said, shrugging. "We were just kidding."

"It didn't sound like kidding to me." Coach narrowed his eyes at Chad. "Plus, a little bird told me that some guys are getting picked on."

"It better not have been Finn that squealed." Chad

gave me a sideways glance.

"It wasn't," Coach said, shaking his head. "And it doesn't matter who it was. It shouldn't be happening. We're all one team." Coach cast his eyes at all of us. "It shouldn't be happening to anyone. Got it?"

Chad, Sanjay, Leo, Theo and Niko all nodded together. "Got it, Coach."

"In fact, I have an idea to make the team stronger." Coach's face broke into a smile.

"Are we all going into the weight room to pump iron?" Chad guessed as he flexed his biceps. "My arms could use another workout."

"No, not that kind of strong." Coach shook his head. "I'm talking about building team spirit. We have to learn how to count on each other."

"How are we going to do that?" Niko asked.

"We're going to have a switch day," Coach Cooper said.

"We're not going to switch partners, are we?" Sanjay raised his eyebrows.

"We sure are." Coach Cooper nodded.

I wondered who I would be paired with in the end. There was only one guy I didn't want to be stuck with.

Coach started splitting up the teams. "Niko, you'll be paddling with Leo today. Sanjay, you and Theo will be in the same boat."

Oh, no, I thought.

"And that only leaves one more team." Coach

smiled at Chad, then he smiled at me. "Chad, say hi to your new partner for the day, Finn."

"But, Coach —" I started to say.

"But, Coach, nothing." Coach shook his head at me. "You and Chad are together today, Finn. Let's get out there and build a stronger team."

All six of us went to pull our kayaks from the racks in the boathouse. Chad and I each grabbed an end of our long boat and carried it down to the dock. Then we put it into the water and lowered ourselves into the cockpits where we sit.

"I'll paddle up front," Chad said. "That's what I'm used to. Besides, I'm the leader of this team."

"Fine by me," I snapped. I was used to paddling from the back when I paddled with Niko. "But Coach never said who the leader was."

Chad stared at me. "Okay, we can both be leaders today."

We pushed away from the dock and began paddling. Chad's blades dipped into the water faster than Niko's. I wasn't used to it. I tried to match his stroke, but couldn't. I was out of sync. Our boat moved from side to side. It wasn't going straight like it should.

"Hey, what's going on?" Chad asked over his shoulder as he paddled.

"I'm just getting used to your stroke rate," I said. "I'll get it in a minute."

"You better," he called back.

We kept paddling, and soon I was able to match Chad's stroke speed. Our paddles were hitting the water at the same time. Our kayak skimmed across the lake. I could see Chad nodding ahead of me.

The other two kayaks pulled up beside us.

"Let's race to the point," Sanjay called out, sitting in the boat with Theo. He pointed at the big rock cliff hanging over the water not far away.

"You're on!" Chad shouted.

All three boats took off for the rock point. Niko and Leo took an early lead, but Chad and I soon caught up. It was neck and neck. It looked like it was going to be a tie. Just as we neared the imaginary finish line, Chad yelled out, "Shoot!"

"What?" I shouted, not knowing what he meant.

"Shoot!" he yelled again. This time he leaned far back and the front end of the kayak lifted up and shot forward across the finish line. We beat the other kayak by a nose.

"You guys were lucky," Theo laughed.

Sanjay nodded. "That was a cool move right at the end, Chad."

"It's called 'shooting' your boat," Chad said. "You use it at the finish line to try to win a close race. That's what the Olympic guys do. It would have been even better if my new partner knew how to do it as well." Chad flicked his hair at me. "Then we really would have shot our boat."

I hated to admit it, but Chad was right. I didn't know how to shoot a boat. But I could see how it could really come in handy to win a race. I had to respect Chad for knowing that trick. He must have done his paddling homework.

We paddled for a while longer. Coach Cooper watched us as we mixed up fast sprinting with slower recovery workouts. After a couple of hours, we headed back to the boathouse.

At the dock, Chad and I lifted our kayak out of the water and put it on our shoulders. We hadn't said much during our training. We focused mostly on our paddling. We made sure we followed Coach's orders. As we carried the kayak back to the boathouse, Chad broke the silence. "You can't let our kidding bug you so much, dude. We're just having fun."

Chad's comment brought back how mad I was at him and the others for picking on me. "How would you like it if your mom left and people joked about it?"

Chad let out a big laugh. "I didn't like it."

I stopped in my tracks. "What are you talking about?"

"My mom left a couple of years ago. She and my dad split up. It happened when we lived in Vancouver, before we moved here. All my friends joked that it was my fault she left. It really bugged me at first, but I got used to it. I knew they were just joking. You can't be such a wuss, Finn."

Paddle Battle

We put our long kayak away in the boathouse. As I pedaled home, I couldn't stop thinking about Chad, and his parents splitting up. Why didn't it bother him anymore? Didn't he care about his mom and dad? Or did it just get easier as time went by? I didn't know the answer. But I wanted to find out, because it sure bugged me.

8 Birthdays and HAIRCUTS

The wheels of my mountain bike twisted and turned along the dirt path high above Lake Okanagan. I gripped my handlebars tight and dodged clumps of sagebrush growing along the trail. The air was fresh with the smell of pine trees scattered along the way. Far below, the lake sparkled blue as the ring Mom loved to wear. Everything seemed to remind me of her.

Taking the cliff route was the fastest way to get to the kayak club from home. Riding so close to the edge was a little risky, but the view was awesome. From up on the cliff, the sailboats and motorboats looked like small toys zipping around the huge lake.

The sky wasn't crystal clear the way it usually was, though. Smoke from wildfires burning hundreds of kilometres north was drifting over the lake. It was amazing how far the smoke could travel. On some days, the sun had a hard time shining through the haze. It looked like a giant orange hanging in a grey mist. There was a lot of talk about the wildfires on the news. As long as they stayed far away, no one was too worried.

Coach Cooper had called a special meeting for everyone, first thing in the morning at the boathouse. I didn't have a clue what it was about. Maybe he was going to kick me off the team for finishing last all the time. Or maybe he was going to switch us into different teams again. I had no idea what he was going to say, but I knew it must be important. The last time Coach called a special meeting was to announce the club was getting six new sprint kayaks. They were the new light-weight carbon fiber kind that all the Olympic paddlers used. He said we couldn't blame our old boats for losing. Coach didn't like excuses.

I coasted down the long hill, past the parking lot where some of the parents were dropping off their kids. After racking my bike on the lower level of the boathouse, I headed upstairs to join the others. Almost every junior paddler was already there. I scanned the meeting room and recognized most of the tanned faces. There were about twenty boys and girls, all aged somewhere between twelve and sixteen. The senior team members had summer jobs and trained later in the day. I pulled up a chair next to Niko and waited for the meeting to start.

Coach Cooper bustled in, wearing his usual blue shorts and white Okanagan Kayak Club tee. He held up a colourful brochure. "Anyone know what this is?"

"Looks like a brochure, Coach," Chad wisecracked.

"Very funny." Coach gave Chad a fake smile. "And what kind of brochure is it?"

Everyone leaned forward to study the photo on the front. "I see a lake, a bunch of cabins and some big, old canoes," Niko said. "So I'd say it was a summer camp for kids."

"Good guess, Niko." Coach nodded his approval. "It's Camp Glassy Lake."

"I've heard of that," Sanjay said. "My cousin goes there during the weekdays and comes home for the weekend all summer. It's about an hour's drive north of here."

Coach nodded at Sanjay. "Well your cousin isn't the only one going to Camp Glassy Lake."

"Who else is going?" Chad asked.

Coach swiveled his head to make sure everyone was listening. "We are."

"What are you talking about?" Chad said. "We don't have time to go to some summer camp just for fun. We have to train for nationals. They're only a couple of weeks away."

"You're exactly right," Coach said, pointing the brochure at Chad. "That's why we're going next Saturday and Sunday."

I wrinkled my forehead. Why were we going to some kid's camp for the weekend instead of paddling here? Looking around the room, I could see I wasn't the only one questioning Coach's decision.

"But I've got a birthday party to go to," Sanjay grumbled.

"My dad is taking me to buy a new bike," Niko groaned.

"And I need to get a haircut," Chad griped as he flicked his long hair out of his eyes.

Coach Cooper held up his hands to quiet the room. "Do you hear yourselves? You all have something else to do, some distraction." He met the gazes of the three loudest complainers. "Whether it's a birthday, a bike or a haircut," then he paused and locked eyes with me. "Or whether you're getting into an argument with your family right here at the club, it all means one thing. You're not focused on what's really important — becoming the best paddler you can be."

"Come on, Coach," Chad snickered. "You'd be distracted too if your teacher showed up."

Niko and Sanjay started to laugh, but were cut short by Coach. "That's enough. Let's leave families out of this." He narrowed his eyes at the two jokers. "Got it?"

Niko nodded. "Got it, Coach."

"Me too," Sanjay said, quietly.

I could feel the stares of everyone else in the room. So Coach knew about me mouthing off to Dad, Ms. Putnam and Madison on the deck. One more reason I was mad they showed up without being invited. It wasn't bad enough that my teammates knew about them, but Coach did too.

Birthdays and Haircuts

Pacing in front of the room, Coach Cooper clapped his hands together to pump us up. "Who wants to make the team going to nationals in Ottawa?"

"We do!" everyone chanted as their hands shot up.

Coach smiled and clapped his hands a second time. "And who wants to totally focus on winning their qualifying races the week before?"

I kept quiet. Everyone but me reached high again. "We do!"

Coach held his arms out wide to get everyone's attention before clapping one final time. "So who wants to go to Camp Glassy Lake for two days? There'll be no birthdays, no bikes, no haircuts and no distractions — just eating, sleeping and paddling."

I didn't really care about becoming the best paddler or making the team going to nationals this year. But if it meant a weekend of not having to be around Ms. Putnam, Madison and my dad, then I was all for it. I might have been last, but I raised my hand and cheered along with everyone else. "We do!"

9 Get Out of TOWN

Dad stood in the living room staring out the window at the front lawn. His hands were on his hips. "With all the rain we've been having, the grass has been growing like weeds."

"Yeah, yeah, I'll get to it." I didn't really feel like cutting the grass, or doing any chores, for that matter. Washing dishes, vacuuming, cleaning my room — they all took energy. I was saving that energy for my paddling workouts. That's all I wanted to do. I didn't care what Dad said about chores teaching me responsibility. I didn't know why Dad couldn't do it, anyway. Before Mom left, she used to help me, but now she's gone. Besides, I knew if I waited long enough, Dad would get someone else to cut the grass.

Suddenly, the sound of a lawn mower roared outside. I glanced out the window and my jaw dropped. It was Madison! She was pushing the lawn mower up and down our front yard. "What's Madison doing here?"

"Oh, yeah, I forgot to mention that Madison is going to cut our grass."

"What!"

"Her mom asked if she could do it because Madison needed the spending money. And I needed the grass cut. So I said yes."

It was bad enough that Ms. Putnam had been over to the house. Now Madison was here too. Before I knew it, they'd be moving in! It was a good thing Coach had asked us to leave for the weekend.

"So can I go away Saturday and Sunday?" I had asked Dad before, but it was like he hadn't heard me.

Dad kept looking blankly out the window. It was as if his mind was a thousand miles away. "What's the name of the camp, again?" Dad said like a robot.

"Glassy Lake. It's about an hour away. We're going up by bus Friday afternoon."

"Oh, yeah, I know exactly where it is. There's a provincial campground at the other end of the lake. We used to go camping and fishing there when you were just a little guy." Dad held his hand out waist high to show how small I had been. "We used to cast our lines in the water, hoping to land a rainbow trout. And sometimes we did." His lips stretched into a thin smile as he remembered.

"I thought the name sounded familiar." I nodded. "But I'm not going there to fish, I'm going to paddle with the rest of the club. Coach wants us to focus on the nationals that are coming up in two weeks. He says we're too distracted by problems with our *families* and stuff." I stressed the word families, but Dad took no notice.

"At least he wasn't talking about our family," Dad said.

I rolled my eyes. "That's exactly what he was talking about. Now Coach thinks I have a problem. And it's all because of you and Ms. Putnam."

"You know I didn't mean for that to happen." Dad stayed quiet for a moment then arched an eyebrow. "Maybe I'll go as well."

My jaw dropped open. "What are you talking about? The camp is only for paddlers. No parents are invited."

"I get that," Dad said. "I mean I might go fishing there while you're gone."

I breathed a small sigh of relief. "What about Ms. Putnam?" I asked. "Aren't you having dinner or going to a movie with her, like you have the past few weekends?"

Dad's face fell, and he turned to me. "Not this weekend. And maybe not any other weekend, either."

"Trouble in paradise?" I mocked. I knew it wasn't a very nice thing to say, but I didn't really care. The sooner Ms. Putnam and Madison were out of my life, the better.

"Tracy wants to take a break from seeing me for a while. That talk we all had on the deck at the kayak club threw her for a loop. She hasn't been the same since you told her it was my fault Mom left."

I thought back to how angry I had been, standing on the deck. How mad I've been for a year now. "Well, wasn't it?"

"It's more complicated than you think, Finn."

"It doesn't seem very confusing to me." The rage boiled over in me again. "You didn't like Mom arguing with you, so you made her leave."

Dad pursed his lips. "Like I told Tracy, that's not the whole story."

"Well what is the story?" I said snidely.

"It's true that your mom and I had been fighting for a while." Dad nodded. "We didn't see eye to eye on a lot of things — what to spend our money on, where to go on vacation. Even little things like what to watch on TV. But that's not the only reason she left."

I stared without blinking, waiting for him to explain. "Then why did she?"

"You know that about a year ago your mom got the job offer she always wanted."

"Something to do with climate change?" I knew Mom had studied that at university and she talked about it a lot. She always said we had to do our part. "Yeah, but I thought she turned it down because we couldn't move out there."

"She did at first." Dad nodded. "But the more time went on, the more she regretted that decision. The job was for the Canadian Centre for Climate Services in Ottawa. They study things like global warming and wildfires. It was a great opportunity for her."

"So Mom left because she wanted to?" I tilted my head, trying to understand. "I thought she took the job because you kicked her out. You didn't make her leave?"

Dad shook his head. "We agreed it was the best thing to do for the two of us."

"What about me?" I snapped. "It wasn't the best thing for me. And now you're trying to make Ms. Putnam my new mom."

"I never thought Tracy was going to replace your mom." Dad's eyes met my cold stare. "But she was good at making me feel less lonely after your mom left. She made me feel better."

I couldn't believe what I was hearing. "What about how lonely I feel?" I fired back. "Do you think getting a text from Mom once a month makes me feel better? It just makes me feel worse."

"Maybe it's not just Tracy and me who need to take a break." Dad put out the palm of one hand as if to make me an offer. "We all need a break, even you and me. Maybe a couple of days apart are just what we need. Then we can start fresh again when we come back, right, buddy?"

"I'm not your buddy," I said, standing up to leave. "And I don't care what you do this weekend. You can go fishing, you can jump in the lake for all I care. I'm going to Glassy Lake with the team so I can get away from you and your girlfriend. That's all I know."

★★★

A while later, the lawn mower stopped and Madison came to the front door. As my dad paid her, she peeked over his shoulder and waved. "Hi, Finn."

I waved back as Dad went into the kitchen.

"I hope you don't mind me cutting your grass," Madison said, wiping sweat off her forehead. "I really need the money."

"What for?" I asked.

"The diving team is competing out of town and I'm saving up. I really want to go." Madison pursed her lips like something was bothering her. "I just need to get away from my mom for a while."

"I know what you mean." I gave Madison a small grin. "I need a break from my dad too."

"I think my mom is also taking a break from your dad for a while. I thought it would make everything all right. But she doesn't look happy about it. She just looks kind of sad."

I nodded. "My dad isn't very happy either."

As Madison walked away, I thought how we were both stuck in the same situation. We were both only kids. Neither one of us had a brother or sister. We both had a parent that had left. Now the parents that had stayed were hardly talking to us. We barely had families anymore.

10 Not Even a RIPPLE

"We must be getting close." Niko pressed his face up against the bus window. We passed a brown, wooden building nestled in thick forest. "There's the warden's office for Glassy Lake Provincial Park."

Coach Cooper turned from his seat at the front of the bus and called out, "Just a few more minutes, everyone."

That announcement got people excited. The gabbing volume on the bus shot up. There were more than twenty paddlers on the bus from the kayak club — about half girls and half boys. Most seats had two paddlers in them, but I made sure I got a spot by myself a couple of rows behind Niko and Chad. I had nothing to say to those guys.

"There it is!" Sanjay shouted. He pointed at the "WELCOME TO CAMP GLASSY LAKE" sign nailed to the trunk of a big pine tree.

The yellow school bus rounded the last corner and came to a rumbling stop in front of a big log cabin.

Pulling in behind us was the pickup truck hauling the long trailer that held all our kayaks. One of the parents had driven, but they'd be heading back to town. It would just be the coaches and the paddlers. We trooped off the bus carrying our gear.

Coach Cooper looked around at all the pine and spruce trees surrounding the camp. He cracked a smile and took a deep breath. "Fresh air — just what we need for a couple of days of tough training."

"I can see why it's called Glassy Lake," Niko said as he gazed out over the crystal-clear water. "There's not even a ripple."

"Yup." Coach nodded. "It's perfect flat water for racing sprint kayaks. Waves won't be slowing you down here. Or the wakes from speed boats. They're not allowed on the lake."

"It's a good thing we brought our own boats," Chad said. "Otherwise we'd have to paddle those relics." He pointed toward the dock where a dozen old canoes had been pulled up on the sandy shore.

"They're classics," Coach said. He walked over to the big blue, green and red boats. "They're the kind of canoes I learned to paddle as a kid when I went to camp."

Niko eyed the colourful boats. "They look a lot wider than what we race in."

"And a lot heavier," I said as I strained to pick up the end of a red canoe.

Coach nodded. "They're a lot more stable for the day campers to paddle. The kids would lose their balance right away in our narrow, light, racing kayaks."

Walking onto the dock, I was able to view the entire lake. It was long and thin as a finger. Somewhere down at the other end was the provincial campground where my dad was fishing. I turned to Coach and held out the backpack and sleeping bag I had been lugging around. "Where do we put our stuff?"

"See those cabins?" Coach flicked his head in the direction of five brown log cabins lined up a little farther along the lake. "Each one has room for four paddlers," Coach explained. "Finn, you'll be staying in cabin three with Niko, Chad and Sanjay."

"Are you sure I'm in with Niko?"

Coach Cooper double checked the list on his tablet. "Of course you are. Niko is your K2 partner. Why wouldn't you be?"

I could see that Coach wasn't about to change plans just for me. "No reason."

Coach waved over Chad, Sanjay and Niko. "Why don't you guys check out your new digs for the weekend and get settled?"

No one had to ask Sanjay twice. Always the keener, he grabbed his bags and headed to cabin three. "Follow me."

Sanjay swung the door open to reveal two bunk beds made from the same logs as the cabin. The whole room smelled of pine.

"I'll take this one," Chad said, climbing to one of the top bunks.

Sanjay threw his gear on the bed under Chad. "This one has my name on it."

Niko made a face. "I guess that just leaves me and you in the other bunks, Finn."

I tossed my sleeping bag onto the lower bed and slumped down.

"Who said you got the bottom bunk?" Niko grumbled.

"Fine, have it your way," I shot back as I climbed the rungs.

The door swung open again and Coach Cooper popped in his head. "Dinner's in the mess hall in fifteen minutes."

"If it's such a mess why are we eating there?" Sanjay asked.

Coach chuckled. "Mess is just a camp word for dining. You know what that means, right?"

Sanjay's eyes lit up. "I've never met a buffet I didn't like."

★★★

Almost two hours later, we stumbled out of the mess hall.

"I've never eaten so many burgers at one meal," Sanjay groaned. "I can barely move."

"Or so many pieces of apple pie," Chad said, patting his stomach.

Coach grinned. "You're going to need that energy tomorrow. The K2 trials are first thing in the morning."

I didn't stuff myself like Sanjay and Chad. It was like they'd never seen an all-you-can-eat buffet before. One cheeseburger and one piece of apple pie were all that I managed to get down, because I wasn't really that hungry. The other guys were stoked to be here and to race to make the nationals team. For me, it was an excuse to be away from the family circus my life had become at home.

There was a loud crack. I jerked my head around. Coach Cooper was by the fire pit, splitting logs with an axe. Niko hurried past me carrying an armful of wood. "We're going to need more logs for the fire, Finn."

"There are lots of other guys who can do that." I shrugged. "Why should I tire myself out?"

"Suit yourself," Niko said. "But you better be pumped tomorrow for our K2 race."

The remaining paddlers straggled out of the mess cabin and wandered over to join us. Heavy log stools made from cut-off tree stumps circled the pit. Each of us took a seat and watched as Coach stacked logs and kindling in the shape of a teepee. My nose burned from the harsh smell of charred ash left over from all the previous campfires.

Coach Cooper lit a match at the base of the logs. Soon, orange and yellow flames were crackling in the growing darkness. Most of the talk was about the next day's paddling. We all knew how important it was to do well if you wanted to make it on the team going to nationals.

"There's no point to anyone else showing up for the U15 race," Chad joked, but we all knew he was serious. "Sanjay and I have it locked up. We haven't been beaten all summer."

In the flickering glow of the fire, I could see Niko's face tighten. "We'll see about that, Chad. All I need is a little help from my partner, and we'll take you." Niko shot me a dirty look.

"Yeah," Leo said from the other side of the pit. "Theo and I aren't here just for the food."

There were a few laughs, but everyone knew how important the next day's races were.

The ring of paddlers fell silent until Coach asked, "Who's got a story?"

11 STORYTIME

As the flames grew higher, the heat from the yellow blaze warmed us in the chilly night air. I peered across the fire to where Sanjay and Chad were sitting on their wooden stumps. Sanjay put up his hand. "I've got a story I don't think everyone's heard, Coach." He looked around the circle at all the girl and boy paddlers who had come on the trip.

"Go ahead, Sanjay." Coach nodded. "We've all just enjoyed a big meal and could use a good story before we hit the hay."

"Oh, it's a good one all right, Coach." Sanjay gave me a sly smile. "In fact, it has something to do with a big meal as well. A big meal at a fancy restaurant with a teacher and someone we all know."

My blood boiled. I wasn't going to let anyone tell this story again. Not in front of the whole club. I was just about to tell Sanjay to shut up when someone beat me to it. Someone I never expected to do it. "Chill, dude," Chad said, grabbing Sanjay's arm. "I don't think everyone wants to hear that story."

"What are you talking about, man?" Sanjay's eyebrows shot up. He stared at Chad in disbelief. "It's the funniest story I've ever heard. Everyone will find it hilarious."

"Not everyone," Chad said, catching my eye across the fire.

Sanjay took a breath. "Okay, Chad, but it was going to be a good one, and you know it."

I took a deep breath as well. My heart was still thumping in my chest. I would have done anything to stop Sanjay from telling that story about Ms. Putnam and me again. I didn't want to leap across the fire pit and tackle Sanjay, but I would have.

Everybody around the circle was staring at Sanjay and Chad. It was easy to see that Sanjay was mad at his kayaking partner. He turned his back on Chad.

"There's nothing to see here," Chad said. His eyes flitted around the circle at the other paddlers. "Why don't we talk about something else? Does anyone else have a story? Leo, Theo, Niko, anyone?" They all shook their heads. Everyone around the campfire went quiet. Finally, a voice broke the silence.

"I have one," Coach Cooper said. He glanced at Chad and Sanjay and gave them a nod. "It's all about getting along with your partner and doing what's best for the team. It's why we had switch day last week."

Now that Coach Cooper was talking, the group

shifted its attention to him.

"It all happened years ago," Coach said, beginning his story. "I was with the Canadian team competing at the Olympic Games in Rio de Janeiro, Brazil. It was the night before our K2 race in the thousand-metre sprint. It was the best event for my partner and me. We even had a chance to medal. I was resting in my room in the Olympic village where athletes from all the different countries stay. Then my phone rang."

Coach paused and stared straight into the crackling fire. His gaze was intense. It was like he was looking at the flame of the Olympic torch.

"It was the head kayaking coach calling. He said my partner had food poisoning from eating some bad pork. He was too sick to race the next day. I couldn't believe it. We had trained so hard for just this one race. My coach said I had a choice. I could either get another partner or not race. But the only other kayaker available was a guy named Troy. Let's just say that I didn't get along with Troy very well. It was a tough decision. But I wasn't a quitter. I wanted to compete in the Olympics. So I decided to race with the guy I didn't like."

Coach almost never talked about himself. We all knew he was a great paddler, but we had never heard this story. Just like everyone else sitting around the fire, I wanted to know what happened. "Did you win, Coach?"

Coach Cooper gave a thin smile and shook his head. "No, we hadn't trained enough together. We didn't want it as a team enough. I wasn't willing to give it my all for him. And he wasn't willing to give it his all for me. You just can't win if you don't believe in each other." Coach shook his head again as he thought back. "We gave it our best shot for Canada, but we came fourth. Just off the podium."

"That's too bad," Sanjay said. "It's unlucky your partner got sick."

"It is, but sometimes bad things happen in life. You just have to deal with them the best you can."

Coach is sure right about bad things happening, I thought. *My mom is gone, and there isn't anything I could have done to stop it.*

"But there is a silver lining to the story," Coach grinned.

"There's a happy ending?" Niko asked.

"You could call it that." Coach nodded. "Once Troy and I got to know each other better, we became good friends. I was even best man at his wedding."

Coach breathed out a long sigh and scanned the faces around the fire circle. "Now, who wants to roast some marshmallows before we turn in for a good night's sleep?"

★★★

As we trudged back to our cabin after the fire, I spotted Chad ahead of me. He was walking by himself.

"What made you do it?" I asked, running to catch up to him.

"What do you mean?" Chad asked blankly.

"You know what," I said. "You stopped Sanjay from telling the story about the restaurant."

"Yeah, so what about it?" Chad said.

"Why'd you do it?" I asked.

Chad stopped in his tracks and looked at me. "Because I knew how you would feel. Because there was a time a story about my mom would have bugged me too. That's all. Let's not make a big deal about it." Chad turned away and kept walking to the cabin.

I stayed behind Chad for the rest of the way, but I felt like we had moved forward.

12 SLEEPLESS

Craaaaack!

A loud crash thundered overhead. Then another. And another. Flashes of piercing light filled the cabin darkness. Black. White. Black. White. I sat bolt upright in my bunk. We had just gone to bed to get some sleep before our big race the next morning.

"What's going on?" Sanjay asked.

Chad cocked his head. "Sounds like a storm."

"And a big one." Niko slid out of bed and stumbled across the floor to turn on the light switch. The cabin stayed pitch black. "Power's out."

I squinted at my phone. "It's almost midnight."

A shadow moved at the bunk across from me. Chad was pulling on his clothes. "Where are you going?" I whisper shouted.

"The sky's lighting up and I want to see it." Chad raced over to the window and peered out. Another crack of lightning lit up the cabin.

"I wonder how far away the storm is," I said.

"Start counting," Sanjay ordered. "And don't stop until I tell you to."

"What for?" I asked.

"Just do it."

I didn't know what Sanjay was talking about, but I began to count. It was Sanjay, after all. "One . . . two . . . three . . ." I kept counting until I got to thirty. Then a low growl of thunder rumbled over our cabin.

"Hear that?" Sanjay asked excitedly.

"Who didn't?" Chad said, as the thunder continued to growl.

"It took thirty seconds for the thunder to get here after the flash of lightning. To find out how many kilometres away the lightning is, all you have to do is divide by three."

I was no math genius, but I could divide thirty by three. "So ten kilometres?"

"Yeah, the lightning is ten kilometres away." Sanjay nodded. "And it's moving farther away from us. The thunder is taking even longer to get here."

"Come on!" Chad shouted, racing to the cabin door. "Let's go!"

Chad flung the door open and sprinted through the darkness toward the dock. I looked at Niko and Sanjay, and they looked back, all of us wondering if we should follow.

"He is my partner," Sanjay said. "I have to go where he goes in the kayak, so I better go now."

All three of us dashed outside and across the grass toward the water. The passing storm had whipped up the wind, which sent cold waves crashing across the dock and over our feet.

Standing on the dock, we could see a long way. I pushed the hair out of my eyes to get a clear view. What I saw left me speechless. In the distant hills, part of the forest was a giant fireball. Red and yellow flames were leaping high into the dark night.

"The lightning must have hit the trees!" Chad shouted, pointing at the flames. "That's awesome!"

"I don't think it's very awesome, dude." Niko shook his head. "Wildfires are just another example of the earth heating up."

"And look what climate change is doing, man." Sanjay flicked his chin at the glowing forest.

"Think of all the trees that fire is destroying," Niko said.

Sanjay nodded. "Not to mention all the birds, deer and other animals running for their lives."

"Just the same," Chad said, still excited, "you don't get to see a wild forest fire every day."

The four of us watched the wildfire burning far away in the distance. While the other guys were thinking about the flames and the forest, I was thinking about my mom. I wondered what her life was like, far away in Ottawa. Did she spend every day thinking about climate change and wildfires? Did she think about me every day or just when she texted, which wasn't very often?

"We should head back," Sanjay said. "It's late."

We ran down the dock and across the grass to the cabin. In the darkness, we climbed back into our bunks.

"We better get some sleep," Niko said, zipping up his sleeping bag.

"You're going to need it," Chad snickered. "But you're never going to beat Sanjay and me, anyway. Right, Sanjay?"

We listened for what Sanjay had to say, but he didn't answer. Sanjay was already fast asleep.

★★★

They call it a sleeping bag, but I don't know why. It should be called a *sleepless* bag, because that's what I was — sleepless. I lay, wide awake, tossing and turning in my bunk with my eyes popped wide open. Then again, maybe it wasn't the bag's fault.

Sanjay's snoring was drifting through the dark cabin straight from his nose to my ears. I rolled over again and checked the time on my phone — 2:15 a.m. *Crap!* There was no way I could doze off with that racket going on. My future didn't look, or sound, good either. In just five hours I had to crawl out of bed and get ready for our big K2 race to qualify for the nationals.

Before coming to the camp, I couldn't have cared less about making the team going to Ottawa. But I was starting to change my mind, especially after listening to Coach's story. He made me realize I owed it to Niko to at least try. I had to be a better teammate. I scrunched my pillow over my head and tried to muffle the sounds coming from below me.

Listening to Sanjay's snuffles wasn't the only reason I lay awake. I was still mad at my dad and my mom. I didn't know which one to blame more. I was angry at Dad for always arguing with Mom. Couldn't they have just gotten along? It probably gave Mom a good excuse to move away for her new job. But how could she just pack up and go to Ottawa? I didn't understand how a family could be three people one day and then only two the next. And did she have to go so far away? Didn't she know how much I wanted her to stay? She still texted me sometimes, but it wasn't the same.

Now that my parents were apart, I thought Dad would be happier. But he wasn't acting that way. He seemed kind of sad now that he and Ms. Putnam were taking a break. I didn't want him seeing Ms. Putnam, but I didn't want him to be unhappy, either. I didn't have any answers to any of my problems. I felt like no one could understand what I was going through.

I rolled over and realized that I wasn't the only one with problems. I guess Madison must have been wondering what was going to happen between her mom and my dad. And Chad had said his mom leaving didn't bug him much anymore, but who could say? Maybe under all that hair it still did.

As I finally drifted off, Sanjay's snoring wasn't the only sound filling the night air. Far off in the distance, I could still hear the crack of lightning and the low rumble of thunder.

13 Wake-Up CALL

A loud buzzing drilled into my foggy brain. Was the sound real or was I dreaming it? Was I awake or was I asleep? I groped around and found my phone. My eyes tried to focus on the time — 7:00 a.m. I blinked, not quite believing I had fallen asleep sometime in the middle of the night. I turned off the alarm and sat up in my bunk. My head felt like it was stuffed with big, white cotton balls.

Chad, Sanjay and Niko were already bustling around the cabin. They were dressed in their shorts and sleeveless racing singlets. They were ready to go.

Chad's eyebrows shot up when he looked at me. "What's wrong with you, dude?"

"What do you mean?" I yawned.

"You look terrible," Niko said. He was wide eyed with concern.

Sanjay did his best to smile at me. "And that's being nice."

I slid down from my top bunk and stumbled across

the floor to the bathroom. The mirror didn't lie — I did look terrible. My hair was matted like the fur of a mangy dog. My bloodshot eyes had sunk into my head, so I looked like the skull on a pirate flag. And my chin was all slimy where I must have drooled in the night. I was a mess. And not the good kind where you eat.

"Let's get some breakfast," Sanjay said eagerly. Somehow he was hungry again after his feeding frenzy the night before.

"And some coffee for Finn." Niko looked me in the eye and grinned. "We might have to pour it right into your mouth."

"But I don't drink coffee," I groaned.

"I don't either, but you're going to start today." Niko nodded. "My mom and dad drink it every morning. They say they can't get going without it."

"Are you sure I need it?" I asked, staring like a zombie.

"Well you need something, but coffee is what we can get," Niko joked. "Our K2 race is this morning and somehow we've got to get you ready for it. Go have a cold shower and we'll meet you in the mess hall."

I turned on the water tap and twisted the dial to cold. I had never taken a cold shower before. *How bad could it be?* I thought. *I stepped under the freezing spray and found out. Yikes! Really bad!* I stayed in for about a minute. The water shot out of the showerhead like tiny icicles. I couldn't take it for another second and jumped out again. I shivered as I toweled off. My arms and legs were covered in goosebumps.

Hair still wet, I trudged into the mess, looking for Niko. I spotted him and slumped into a chair next to the other guys from our cabin. All I wanted to do was sleep. I put my head down on the table and closed my eyes.

"Finn, wake up!" Niko poked my shoulder.

I tried to open one eye.

"Your eyes are like slits," Niko said. "You look like some kind of reptile."

I raised a lizard eyelid. "What?" I said groggily.

"You fell asleep, bro." Niko peered down at me.

"No, I didn't." I tried to shake my head, but the table stopped it from moving.

"Yeah, you did, seriously." Niko nodded once, hard.

It took all the energy I had to lift my head off the table. Then, I put my elbows next to my knife and fork and rested my chin on my hands. My eyes still wouldn't open.

"Here, eat this," Niko said. He slid a plate in front of me. It was stacked high with food from the buffet table. "I loaded it up for you."

Even with my eyes half closed, I could smell what was on the plate. I breathed in the aroma of pancakes, waffles, bacon and scrambled eggs, all smothered in maple syrup. My stomach lurched.

"I'm too tired to eat," I whispered.

"You're eating," Niko insisted. He stabbed a piece of waffle with his fork and shoved it between my lips.

My mouth was having a hard time chewing, but I managed to get down a pancake, half a waffle and a piece of crispy bacon. "I can't eat another bite."

"Here," Niko said as he poured me a cup of steaming black coffee. "You're going to need this as well."

I took a sip. "That's gross!"

Niko laughed. "Add some milk and sugar."

To make it less bitter, I stirred in a big spoonful of sugar. I was just about to reach for the cup again when a big hand swooped in and took it away.

"Not so fast, Finn." Coach Cooper was standing over me. "That's not for you or any other junior paddler. Coffee is only for the adults." He checked the other cups on the table to make sure no one else was drinking coffee. "I don't know why you would need it, anyway." Coach arched an eyebrow. "I'm sure everyone went to bed early to get a good night's rest for the races this morning, right?"

Coach Cooper carried my full coffee cup over to the counter, then walked to the front of the room. He held up his hands to make an announcement. "Listen up, everyone. We'll be unloading the boats in fifteen minutes. Don't be late."

Niko slapped me on the back. "I'll meet you by the trailer to get our kayak, Finn." Then he joined the other paddlers streaming out of the mess hall. Soon, I was left sipping a glass of orange juice by myself. The races hadn't even started yet and I was already trying to catch up. I should have known better.

The night before I had been mad at my mom and dad. This morning I was mad at myself for not getting more sleep. I knew I had a big race. I knew I had to help Niko. I might not have been able to change what was going on between my parents. But I could change how ready I was to compete. I had to. Next time I'd try not worry so much. If there was a next time.

14 A Hazy START

Shuffling out of the mess hall, I was met by a blanket of haze hanging over the lake. The thunderstorm had passed, but a smoky fog had rolled in overnight. I rushed over to the trailer, feeling bad that I was late. I knew the unloading would almost be finished. Taking the kayaks off the trailer was a big job and we were all expected to help. But when I got there, not a single boat had been removed. A blue pickup with an official park warden crest on the door had just pulled in. Niko, Chad, Sanjay and the rest of the paddlers were gathered around listening to a man in a brown shirt and green pants.

"This is Warden Tailfeathers." Coach Cooper nodded at the man standing next to him wearing a wide-brimmed hat. A long, black braid hung down his back. "He has some important news. Everyone, listen up."

"You'll notice there's a fair amount of smoke in the air this morning," the warden said as he scanned the grey sky. "That's from a new wildfire burning about fifty kilometres north of here, toward Kamloops. There was a lightning strike last night and the forest is so tinder dry, it lit up like a match."

Chad nodded at Sanjay and Niko as they remembered watching the flames from the dock.

"What does that mean for us here on Glassy Lake, Warden?" Coach asked.

I wondered the same thing. My dad was camping not far away. If there was a lightning strike, he'd be right in the path of another wildfire. Even though I was sleepy, I listened carefully.

"There's no danger right now," Warden Tailfeathers said. He held up both hands to reassure us. "It's still a long way away. We've got firefighting crews trying to control the blaze. But you never know with Mother Nature. There could be more lightning strikes here in the Glassy Lake area. And that could mean more wildfires."

Coach's brow wrinkled with concern. "Then what?"

"Then you'd have to be ready to evacuate. Things could get really dangerous, really fast. You'd have to leave camp right away. I'll let you know."

Warden Tailfeathers cast a serious look over our group, then a smile crept over his face. "But don't worry about it today. I can see you're here to kayak on beautiful Glassy Lake. There's a little smoke in the air, but nothing to worry about. I hope everyone has a great day paddling."

We watched the warden's pickup drive away. Then we got ready to unload the trailer.

Niko untied one of the nylon straps holding our kayak. "Help me grab our boat, Finn."

I lifted the other end of the kayak, but yawned and lost my grip for a split second.

"Careful!" Coach shouted. "These boats are fragile, not to mention expensive."

After I got a better grasp, we carried the long, sleek, sprint kayak down to the water's edge. Still feeling groggy, I had to watch my step so I didn't stumble and send our boat crashing to the ground. Dropping one could easily result in a dent or crack. The rest of the paddlers followed right behind us with their boats. Half an hour later, there was a rainbow of more than twenty brightly coloured kayaks lined up along the shore.

Coach Cooper stood on the dock holding a white flag. He spoke to the big group of paddlers gathered on shore. "Today is the big day. We've got a lot of races lined up, and every one is important. The winner of each race will qualify for the team going to the nationals next week in Ottawa."

Niko's face fell. "What if we don't win?"

"Then I'm afraid you don't qualify for the team," Coach said, shaking his head. "Only the best get to go."

I could hear some of the boys and girls grumbling around me.

"The club has the money to send only so many paddlers," Coach Cooper explained. "We'd love to bring everyone, but we just can't afford it. It's expensive when you add up the plane tickets, hotel rooms and all the meals."

"Yeah, especially if Sanjay goes," Chad wisecracked, making fun of his partner's huge appetite.

Coach scanned the hazy lake. "As the warden said, there's smoke in the air, but other than that we have perfect conditions for racing. There's no wind, the water is calm and the course is marked. There's nothing else to worry about — no birthdays, no haircuts, no distractions. All you have to do is focus on having your best race."

No birthdays and no haircuts, but what about no sleep? I thought. *Coach forgot to mention that one.*

"The first event this morning is the K2, thousand-metre race for U15 boys," Coach said, checking the list on his tablet.

"First, all right." Chad shot me a sly look. "Hope everyone's awake."

Niko met my sleepy eyes. "Don't worry about Chad. I'm sure the waffles will give you all the energy you need. You'll be fine, Finn."

I grimaced and nodded weakly, before turning my attention to Coach again.

"To start every race, I'll wave this flag." Coach raised the white flag high over his head. "The finish

line is even with the dock that I'm standing on."
He pointed at the floating buoys marking the lanes
on the water. "The first team to reach me will be the
winner."

Coach looked over the big group of paddlers one
more time in case anyone had any last-minute questions.
No hands were raised. We were all ready to go. Coach
clapped his hands together a couple of times. "Good
luck, everyone, and may the best teams win."

Niko and I slipped our kayak into the lake and
began paddling toward the starting line a thousand
metres away. The water was cement grey, just like the
sky. You couldn't tell where one stopped and the other
began. The other two boats glided along right beside
us. There was an eerie silence between us. No one said
a word.

Our blades moved through the water slowly to save
energy for the real race. My arms were already dead
tired. The paddle felt as heavy as a barbell from the
weight room. I kept stroking, hoping my arms would
warm up.

All three kayaks spotted the red buoy Coach had
used to mark the starting line. We paddled so the tips
of our boats were lined up with it. We were set. All we
needed now was the signal. I peered through the smoky
haze, trying to see Coach drop the white flag to start
the race.

15 HANG ON

"There it is!" Niko shouted over his shoulder. "Coach dropped the white flag."

"Are you sure?" I strained my eyes to see through the grey haze.

"Let's go!" Chad yelled to Sanjay from their kayak on our left.

"Come on!" Leo urged Theo on our right.

I wasn't sure if Coach had waved his white flag, but I couldn't wait another second. The other two kayaks were charging ahead. The race was on.

"What are you waiting for?" Niko screamed back at me. He had already started paddling as fast as he could, trying to catch the two boats pulling away.

Hearing Niko shout snapped me out of my daze. A shot of adrenalin pulsed through me. This was my only chance to make up for letting him down. I couldn't let one sleepless night be an excuse. I dug my paddle into the water and pulled hard.

Water sprayed as I matched Niko's stroke.

Our blades hit the water at the same time, shooting us forward into the mist. Even though the smoke wasn't thick, my eyes still burned. I was already breathing hard, and wondered if the smoke would slow me down. It didn't seem to be bothering the other two kayaks. They were blasting ahead of us.

Niko and I pulled our blades through the water, giving everything we had. I started to feel better. My arms weren't so rubbery. My shoulders weren't so tight. My back didn't ache like it had when I creaked out of bed.

I checked Leo's green boat on our right. He fired a look straight back. His face was strained with the fierce effort of the battle. Little by little, Niko and I were catching up. Our start had been terrible, but we were almost even with the other kayak. Stroke . . . stroke . . . stroke. We were pulling ahead.

Chad and Sanjay were dead ahead on our left. Chad sat in the front cockpit, Sanjay behind him. Both were paddling as hard as they could. Neither one even glanced at us. That was our chance. They were so focused on paddling, they might not notice our boat coming up fast.

Niko's arms were thrust forward. His blades churned through the water. Drops of sweat flew from his hair. My arms were wet with a mix of sweat and spray from the lake. We paddled like it was our last race of the season. It would be if we didn't win.

Images flashed through my head. I thought of my dad. How angry I was at him for splitting up with my mom. How I didn't want Ms. Putnam or Madison coming to dinner, coming to my kayak club, coming into my life. I plunged my blade in the deep water and pulled.

I thought of my mom. How I was mad at her too. How could she just pack up and move away to a new city? Was a job more important than me? I gripped my paddle hard and poured my rage into every stroke.

Now the tips of our boats were even. We were red and blue arrows flying side by side down the course. That got Chad's attention. He shot us a sideways glance. That was the look I wanted to see. The face of panic. The face that realized we weren't going to give up. That we wanted to win just as much as they did. That Chad and Sanjay were in the race of their lives.

I started to believe we could do this. That Niko and I could be a great team. That I could be the partner he wanted me to be. That we could trust each other, just like Coach said. I could see Niko believed it too. His strokes were fast and smooth. His effort was relentless.

We surged ahead.

Then it started. It began as a twinge in my right arm. *What is that?* I thought. Something felt off. I tried to ignore it, but the pain kept coming back. My bicep began to hurt. A dull throbbing spread across my shoulders. My back began to spasm. My whole body was tightening up. *This can't be happening!* I thought.

"Not now!" I cried out.

Niko whipped his head around and saw me grimace. "We're almost there, Finn!"

Coach stood on the dock just a hundred metres away. The white flag was hanging at his side. My heart pounded — partly from the stabbing pain and partly from the dread of knowing I might not make it. My body was giving out. My energy was crashing from lack of sleep.

If I can just hang on a few more strokes, I thought.

The finish line was so close I could almost touch it. Coach raised his arm, ready to drop the flag as the winning boat sped by.

This is it! I thought. I thrust my paddle in the water one more time, but it would be my last. My arms froze. My back seized. I had squeezed every last drop of fuel from my tired body. Now my tank was empty. I collapsed, my head falling forward against the kayak.

I felt faint, like it was all a dream. Chad and Sanjay flashed by us. The brothers Leo and Theo skimmed across the water right behind. Niko kept paddling, but it was no use. We fell to third.

Chad yelled out, "Shoot!" He and Sanjay leaned back and their boat shot across the finish line. The blur of a white flag waved on the dock. The race was over.

Niko's chest was still heaving when he turned to me.

I expected him to be angry. He deserved to be mad. I had let him down again.

"We almost did it, Finn," he said.

I stared at Niko blankly through half-open eyes. Why wasn't he yelling at me? Why wasn't he smashing his paddle into the water? He had wanted to go to nationals a lot more than I did. He must have been disappointed. I knew I would be if I were him.

Then a slow smile crept across my partner's sweaty face. "You gave everything you had," Niko said between breaths. "But you just ran out of gas."

Niko put down his paddle and reached out his fist. A knuckle bump wasn't the same as winning a spot on the team going to Ottawa, but I'd take it. Niko was a great teammate and a true friend.

Coach Cooper helped us pull our boats out of the water and lay them on the dock. "What a race!" he said, wide eyed. "First, I thought Niko and Finn had it, but then Chad and Sanjay beat out Leo and Theo at the line." He turned to the winning team. "Congratulations, Chad and Sanjay — you guys are off to the nationals."

I could see Niko's shoulders slump with defeat.

"Sorry, man," I said. "I know you wanted to win."

"No need to apologize." Niko's face brightened as he met my eyes. "For the first time in a long time, I know you wanted to win just as much as I did."

16 MISSING

After the race, I trudged back to the cabin for a rest. I couldn't remember if I had ever been so tired. I fell asleep as soon as my head hit the pillow.

Two hours later I was jolted awake. A vehicle was speeding into the camp. Still half asleep, I stumbled toward the parking lot, almost tripping over the old canoes on the grass. Overhead, the sky was growing darker. Big clouds had rolled in. The wind was blowing in the trees. Branches were swaying. Another storm was coming.

The blue pickup skidded to a stop on the gravel and the warden hopped out. Chad and Niko were already there. Coach Cooper rushed from the mess hall. The rest of the paddlers quickly gathered around the truck.

"What's going on, Warden Tailfeathers?" Coach asked.

"Glassy Lake Provincial Park has been hit by lightning." The warden's voice was calm but stern. "The strike started a wildfire that's sweeping through the park. It's growing every minute."

Am I hearing that right? I wondered. *Did the warden say Glassy Lake Provincial Park? That's where my dad is!*

"Is there any way to control it?" Coach asked.

The warden looked doubtful. "Help is on the way. They're sending water bombers and helicopters to fight the blaze. But it's Mother Nature at work. And she usually can't be stopped."

"That doesn't sound good," Coach said. "The fire is a few kilometres away at the other end of the lake. Are we safe here?"

Warden Tailfeathers shook his head firmly. "It's not safe to be anywhere in the area. The wind could shift the direction of the fire at any moment. It's time to pack up and leave, Coach."

Coach Cooper raised both hands to get the attention of all the boys and girls. "You heard what the warden said. It's time to leave. Everyone go back to your cabin and get your things together. Then meet at the bus. Let's move!"

I rushed beside Warden Tailfeathers. "Did you say lightning hit the provincial park?"

"I sure did, son." The warden locked eyes with me. "Do you know someone camping there?"

"My dad!"

"I'll check on him," Warden Tailfeathers said. "But you should call him to make sure he leaves."

I raced back to the cabin and grabbed my phone. I tapped Dad's number and waited. "Come on," I said out loud. There was no answer. I tried one more time, but there was still no answer. I was just about to try for a third time when the cabin door flew open.

"Is Sanjay in here with you?" Chad shouted. His face was tight with panic.

"No," I said. "I thought he was with you."

"He's missing!" Chad said. "We have to find him."

We ran back to the mess hall. No Sanjay. Then we sprinted down to the dock. "Sanjay's single kayak is gone!" Chad yelled.

"He must have gone for a paddle by himself," I said. "He was probably still excited after winning the race."

"I have to find him right away." Chad eyed the choppy water on the lake. "And I need your help, Finn."

I ran with Chad toward the two-man kayaks we had just raced in that morning. "Let's take the K2," Chad said.

"It's too narrow and too tippy for the rough water," I shouted. "And too small — we'd never be able to fit Sanjay in the boat if we had to."

We rushed toward the old canoes that were lined up on the grass. "Grab the bow of the red one," Chad said, pointing to the front of the boat.

"What about our life belts?" I said. It could be

deadly to go without them. My eyes searched the inside of the canoe as I picked up the end of the heavy boat. Two wooden paddles and two lifejackets had been left in the bottom. "We're good!" I yelled.

"Where are you guys going?" Coach shouted, running up to us.

"Sanjay is missing," Chad said. "We're going to look for him."

"We have to find him fast!" Coach nodded. "I'll take another big canoe. I'll be right behind you."

Chad lifted the back of the canoe and we carried it down to the water's edge. We hopped in. Soon our blades were digging into the lake, stroking through the water. Now Chad and I were racing on the same team. But this time we were racing to find Sanjay.

We leaned forward and paddled into the teeth of the wind. We kept our eyes peeled for Sanjay, calling out his name as we stroked. "Sanjay! Saaanjaaay!"

Cold spray from the cresting waves lashed our faces with every stroke. Whitecaps this big would have been too much for our sprint kayak. Our sleek racing boat would have capsized, tipping us into the cold water. We would have had to cling to the sides until help arrived. I wondered if that had happened to Sanjay. Was he somewhere out there in the stormy waters?

17 Search TEAM

We pressed on through the grey mist. Our eyes stung from the smoke. Chad's blade pulled through the water on the left side, mine on the right. Our blades hit the water at exactly the same time. We stroked together like we had been a team for years. We paddled as if it was life and death. And it was — Sanjay's life.

The old canoe handled like a huge tanker. Despite paddling as hard as we could, the boat didn't knife through the water like our sleek kayak would have. The big canoe was twice as wide and twice as stable. It was the only boat that had a chance of making it through the rough waves. I looked behind us and saw Coach paddling hard to catch up.

A loud roar growled behind us. I turned my head but saw nothing along the water. The roar continued. *Where is the sound coming from?* I thought. I glanced in the sky and my heart jumped. A big plane with wide wings and large propellers was flying straight for us! *Must be a water bomber*, I thought. And it was getting lower as if it was coming in to land.

"There's a plane behind us!" I screamed.

"What?" Chad kept paddling. "There's *rain* behind us?"

"No, a plane!" I shouted.

Chad's head spun and his eyes bulged. "Do you think he sees us?"

"There's too much smoke," I yelled. "If we don't move he's going to smash us. We have to get out of the way!"

I waved at Coach and pointed at the plane speeding toward us. He nodded then pointed at the shore.

We turned our canoe sharply toward the rocky shore and kept paddling like mad. Both our boats had to get out of the bomber's runway.

My stroke rate spiked. My breaths were short. My chest heaved. *This must be what a heart attack feels like,* I thought. We didn't stop paddling until we heard the loud woosh of the bomber on the lake behind us. We looked back and watched the big plane scoop up water as it skimmed along the surface of the lake. It didn't even stop. Then the water bomber took off. It climbed steeply through the smoky air and headed toward the burning forest at the end of the lake.

Still catching our breaths, we grabbed our paddles and continued on our mission. We were tired, but we had to keep giving all we had. Sanjay was out there somewhere. I gritted my teeth and thrust my paddle back into the water.

"What's that over there?" Chad pointed straight ahead of us.

"It's a kayak!" I shouted. "But there's nobody in it."

With a burst of energy, Chad launched his blade into the swirling water and pulled with all his might. I matched his stroke and we knifed through the waves to the empty kayak.

"Sanjay!" I called out. But he was nowhere to be seen.

"I'm over here!" Sanjay yelled. His head popped up over the kayak. He was hanging on to the other side.

"Let's get him into your canoe," Coach called out from behind us.

We paddled beside Sanjay and hauled him into our boat. He sat slumped over, holding his arm. He was shivering.

"What happened?" Chad asked, leaning forward with concern.

"My paddle hit a log that was under the water," Sanjay said, wincing. "I didn't even see it."

"It must have burned in the fire and fallen into the lake," Coach said.

"My arm hurts real bad," Sanjay groaned. "I can't move it."

"Let's get you back to camp," Coach said. "Follow me."

The wind kept howling as we paddled, but soon we were back at the dock. Coach Cooper helped Sanjay out of our canoe.

"Sorry, Coach," Sanjay said, still holding his arm. "I know I shouldn't paddle alone. I was just so excited about going to nationals."

"I know, Sanjay." Coach nodded. "The important thing is that you're safe."

We walked quickly toward the bus that had waited for us. We knew we had to leave as soon as possible. The wildfire was still heading toward the camp.

"How's your arm, Sanjay?" Chad asked. "Do you think you'll be able to paddle at the nationals next week?"

"It doesn't feel good, man." Sanjay shook his head and groaned again. "It really hurts."

"What are we going to do, Coach?" Chad asked. "There's no way Sanjay can paddle in Ottawa."

Coach watched Sanjay hold his injured arm and thought for a moment. "Looks like you're going to need another partner, Chad."

"What do you think about this guy right here?" Chad flicked his head at me.

"I think Finn would be a great choice," Coach said. "You guys just proved you know how to work together when the going gets tough. And the nationals are tough."

I made sure Sanjay was safely on the bus. Then I ran

back to the cabin to get his gear and mine. The wildfire was closing in. There was no time to waste. I picked up my phone to try calling my dad one more time. I had to warn him.

There was a text message.

No fun fishing without you, Finn. I left early. See you at home — Dad.

I pocketed my phone and breathed a sigh of relief. My mom was gone. I couldn't lose my dad as well. We had to find a way to get along. I could tell he cared about me. With Ms. Putnam out of the picture he might even need me. One thing was for sure. I needed him.

18 ROOMMATES

"There are the Parliament buildings!" I pointed out the bus window as we drove by the old stone buildings with the green roofs.

We had just landed at Ottawa's International Airport and were driving with the rest of our BC team to the hotel. Sanjay was back home with his arm in a sling. I just hoped I could be as good a paddling partner for Chad as he was. Dad and the other parents were staying nearby in another hotel. Coach Cooper thought it was better that way. He said it would help us focus while we were at the national championships. Dad and I didn't sit together on the plane. I was in a big group with Chad and the rest of the team. I was glad he came on the trip, though. He didn't get to watch me compete very often. We planned to meet at the race the next morning.

"That's one tall building." Chad peered up at the Peace Tower with the clock and the flag flying at the top. "I bet you could see a long way from up there."

We drove through downtown Ottawa, past some

big buildings. A lot of them had signs with the Canadian maple leaf on them to show they were government offices. I wondered if my mom did her climate change work in one of them.

The bus parked in front of the hotel. We grabbed our bags and met in the lobby. The hotel was buzzing with activity. There were young kayakers and canoers everywhere.

"This must be the hotel where all the athletes are staying." Chad spun around like a top to view everybody.

"There'll be hundreds of kids just like us from all over Canada," I said as some girl paddlers from Ontario walked by wearing their club jackets.

Coach Cooper was one of the coaches overseeing the BC team. He waved us over. "Chad and Finn, you'll be rooming together. You have a big day tomorrow. Your K2 race is one of the first ones scheduled in the morning. Make sure you get a good night's rest."

I remembered the last time Coach said that at Camp Glassy Lake. I had hardly slept at all. Worrying about my dad, thinking about my mom, listening to Sanjay snore and the thunderstorm rage kept me awake almost the whole night. I hoped tonight would be different.

After a big spaghetti dinner in the hotel restaurant, Chad and I took the elevator up to our room.

"Here it is," Chad said. He slid the card key into the slot, then pushed open the door.

We unpacked and then sat on our beds. I wasn't sure what to say. On the plane ride, Chad and I hadn't spoken too much. We mostly watched movies on the small screens in front of us. Even though Chad had stopped Sanjay from telling the restaurant story and I had helped him rescue Sanjay, we still didn't know each other very well. We weren't best friends or anything.

"So your dad came on the trip?" I asked Chad.

"Yeah, my dad, but not my mom." Chad nodded. "They don't do much together."

"I know what you mean," I said. "I asked my dad if we could see my mom while we were in Ottawa. But he said we were only here for two days and there wouldn't be time. I think he just didn't want to see her." I let out a long sigh. "I even texted her to say we were coming, but she never wrote back."

"That's rough," Chad said, lying back on the bed. "I know that you miss her."

I nodded slowly. "Don't you miss your mom?"

"Sometimes." Chad pushed a hand through his hair. "But I'm used to it. I still see her on holidays, my birthday and things like that."

"So you're not mad at her for leaving?"

"Not anymore." Chad shook his head. "I was at first. But being mad wasn't making me feel any better. Something had to change."

I tilted my head, wondering. "What was that?"

"Me." Chad smiled. "I had to change." He spread out his

hands to explain. "I realized that's just the way it was. I knew my mom still cared about me. She just didn't care much about my dad. I'm pretty sure it happens to other kids too."

"You got that right." I nodded, remembering back to when my mom and dad argued all the time. "I guess it's better they're not together."

"And it's better for you that they're not together," Chad said. "Our house is a lot more peaceful now. I don't have to listen to them fighting. It lets me focus on the things I like to do."

"Like kayak racing," I said, grinning.

Chad cracked a smile as well. "You got it, dude."

After we had brushed our teeth, we climbed into our beds.

"I'm beat," Chad said, letting out a big yawn. "Flying to big national championships and staying in fancy hotels always makes me tired," he joked as if it happened all the time.

We set the alarms on our phones to make sure we got up early. We couldn't be late for our race. Then Chad turned out the light. "We're a lot more alike than you might think, Finn," he said in the darkness. "We make a good team."

I rolled over and closed my eyes. I thought about what Chad had said. How he just got used to his mom and dad being apart. How it was better for everyone. I took a deep breath and started to relax. I knew he was right about his family. Maybe he was right about mine too.

19 Spin AROUND

The next morning, Chad and I hopped on another bus. We sat with the rest of the BC team going to the competition. There were boys and girls of all ages, from even younger than we were all the way up to paddlers in their twenties. Some were even trying to make it to the Olympics. There was a lot of excited chatter. Everybody was pumped for the championships.

After a fifteen-minute drive, we got to Mooney's Bay on the Rideau Canal. That was where all the races would be held.

"Let's meet at the BC tent in fifteen minutes," Coach Cooper announced from the front of the bus. "I'll give you any last-minute instructions before you head out on the water for your races."

We jumped off the bus and scanned the area. The first thing we saw was the canal. It was huge, just like a wide river. The racecourse had been marked into nine lanes with long strings of white buoys. There were already kayaks and canoes out on the water warming up. The races would be starting soon.

Down by the water was a big clubhouse that would be the headquarters for the competition. It was a lot bigger than our clubhouse back in Kelowna. Nearby was the group of white tents that Coach had mentioned. There was one for each province. We could see the BC flag on one of them. That was where we would meet. A little farther on were the viewing stands that overlooked the finish line for all the races. The bleachers had a lot of seats — there must have been a thousand or more!

Chad and I grinned as we walked under a big banner that said "WELCOME TO THE CANADIAN SPRINT NATIONAL CHAMPIONSHIPS." There were hundreds of people everywhere. Some were carrying canoes and kayaks. Some were still eating breakfast. Some were looking for their families. That's what we were doing.

"There's my dad!" Chad waved at a man in the distance. "I'll meet you at the tent in a few minutes to get ready for our race."

I nodded and searched the busy grounds for my dad. There was no sign of him. *I'm sure we agreed to meet at eight o'clock*, I thought.

Then I felt a tap on my shoulder. I spun around. "Dad!"

"I'm glad I found you," Dad said with a big smile on his face. "I wanted to make sure I got the chance to wish you good luck."

"I'm glad I found you too." Dad and I had been getting along better since we had both made it back safely from Glassy Lake. I didn't blame him so much for Mom leaving. I realized she had left for more reasons than just him. But Dad was still kind of sad. I think not seeing Ms. Putnam had something to do with that. "I only have a few minutes before the race," I said.

"This is a big deal, Finn." Dad craned his neck around to take in all the action. "The best paddlers are here from all over Canada." He met my eyes. "I'm very proud of you, son."

I couldn't remember the last time Dad said he was proud of me. It felt good to hear. "Thanks, Dad." But my smile wasn't as big as it could have been. Part of me still wasn't happy.

Dad studied my face. "What's the matter, Finn?"

I paused. "It's just too bad Mom couldn't be here to watch me race too."

"I'm sure your mom is very busy with work," Dad said. We both knew he was making an excuse.

"But she's not too busy to watch her son," said a woman behind me. It was a voice I'd recognize anywhere. It was a voice I hadn't heard in almost a year.

I spun around again. This time Mom was standing right in front of me.

"Mom!" I said. "You came!"

"I sure did." Mom's face lit up. "I didn't text you I

was coming because I wasn't sure that I could make it. I've been away at a big climate change conference in Paris. But I left early."

I raised my eyebrows. "Just to come back and watch me?"

Mom nodded. "I couldn't miss seeing you compete in the biggest race of the year, could I? And I wanted to say hello to your dad too," she added, turning to Dad. "It's good to see you, Blake."

I watched my dad and wondered what he would say. I didn't know if he was still mad at her.

"It's good to see you as well, Grace." Dad gave her a warm smile. "You look happy."

"I am." Mom grinned back. "This is the best job I've ever had. It feels like I'm doing something really important. Like I'm helping the world be a better place."

I was surprised that Mom and Dad seemed to be getting along. But it was good to see. It was a lot better than the last time they were together. I still remembered Mom slamming the front door behind her as she carried her bags out to the taxi on the street. That was the worst.

"It's been harder and busier than I thought to settle in here. But I need to be a better mom, Finn." Mom met my eyes. "I promise to text you more often. Come for visits when I can. Maybe you can even come to Ottawa and we can go on a tour of the Parliament buildings."

"Really?" I asked, not quite believing what I was hearing.

"Really." Mom squeezed my arm just like she used to.

"I'd like that," I said.

Dad looked at his watch. "Don't you have a big race this morning, Finn?"

"The biggest." I snapped back to thinking about the race. "And I'm paddling with a new partner. I don't know how we'll do, but we're going to try our best."

"That's all any of us can do," Dad said, patting me on the back. "Sometimes we get new partners."

Mom smiled at me and then at Dad. "All we can do is try our best."

20 Finish LINE

The race was only seconds away. I sat behind Chad as we floated in our kayak at the starting line. Our muscles were tense. Our eyes focused straight down the thousand-metre course. The sky was blue, not a whiff of smoke in the air. I took a deep breath.

At the finish line, a large crowd was watching from the stands. A podium stood nearby where the medal ceremonies would take place. Next to the three steps was a large flame that burned like the Olympic torch. A man's voice boomed through speakers to announce the race.

"IN LANE ONE: ONTARIO, LANE TWO: BRITISH COLUMBIA, LANE THREE: ALBERTA . . ."

We were sandwiched between the two best teams in the country. But we didn't have time to get scared by the competition. Everything was happening in a blur. The week before, we had been competing at Camp Glassy Lake with wildfires burning around us. Now we were here at the Canadian national championships in Ottawa waiting for the biggest race of our lives.

The starting horn blared. We were off.

Chad and I dug our paddles deep into the water at the same time. Our kayak shot forward. Coach Cooper had told us to start fast. He said the first ten strokes were the most important. We had to take short strokes to get up to top speed as quickly as we could. Coach's plan was working. We were out in front. No boats to our left. No boats to our right.

"BRITISH COLUMBIA IS OUT FAST AND HAVE TAKEN AN EARLY LEAD."

My stroke rate was high, but not as rapid as my pulse. The beating inside my chest felt like a jackhammer. But I knew the thumping would calm down as my muscles warmed up and we settled into the race.

My confidence grew with every stroke. "We can do this, Chad!"

Chad said nothing. He didn't have to. The way he attacked the race, the way his strong arms pulled his blades through the water, said it all. We skimmed across the canal like it was a sheet of glass.

I glanced at lane one to my right. I could see the tip of a boat from the corner of my eye.

"ONTARIO IS CHALLENGING IN LANE ONE."

I glanced to my left.

"AND ALBERTA IS COMING ON STRONG

IN LANE THREE. LOOKS LIKE WE'VE GOT A THREE-WAY RACE, FOLKS."

This wasn't going to happen again. There was no way I was going to let two other boats catch and pass us. I didn't know how we could paddle any faster, but we had to try.

"Let's go, Chad!"

Sweat drenched Chad's shirt as he upped his stroke rate. White water sprayed from our blades as we knifed between the buoys that lined our lane. We did everything we could to stay ahead of the other two boats. But it wasn't enough.

"ONTARIO AND ALBERTA HAVE CAUGHT THE BOAT FROM BRITISH COLUMBIA, AND THEY'RE INCHING AHEAD."

I started to wonder if we were as good as the other two teams. Chad and I had trained together for a week. But maybe that wasn't enough. We had practised shooting our boat at the finish. But maybe we needed more. We had learned to trust each other. But maybe it was too late.

"THE RACE IS MORE THAN HALF OVER. I DON'T KNOW IF THE BOYS FROM BC CAN RECOVER."

The kayaks from Ontario and Alberta were surging ahead. Now their stroke rate was faster than ours. We couldn't keep up. We had given everything we had for the first half of the race and were tiring. The finish line was only five-hundred metres away. I could see the bleachers where all the spectators were watching. And I could see the flame burning bright in its silver cauldron.

The flame reminded me of the wildfires at the camp. How Chad and I had paddled through the smoke and choppy water to rescue Sanjay. *If we can race through that, we can race through anything*, I thought. *Nothing can stop us.*

"The flame!" I shouted.

Chad shot a glance at the yellow torch by the podium. Coach's fireside story burned in my memory. I'm sure Chad remembered too. We both knew the power of the Olympic flame.

That's all it took. We started paddling with the same fury as we had a week before. Every stroke was like we were paddling to save Sanjay. My heart pounded. My arms ached. We surged ahead.

"BC HAS COME BACK! THE THREE BOATS ARE NECK AND NECK."

We were side by side with the other two kayaks. If we could only pull ahead.

The finish line was getting close. The crowd was cheering.

"Come on, Finn!" a man called out.

That's my dad! I thought.

"You can do it, Finn!" a woman yelled as loud as she could.

And my mom! They're cheering for me, together.

I put my head down. I didn't know how the race was going to end. But I was going to give it my best. We flew forward.

"THIS IS GOING TO BE CLOSE! HERE COMES THE FINISH LINE!"

There were only a few more strokes to go. We knew what to do if it was a close race at the finish line. We had practised the move all week. It was now or never.

"Shoot!" Chad shouted.

On our very last stroke, Chad and I both leaned back. The bow of our kayak lifted out of the water and shot forward. We crossed the finish line, not knowing if we had won, come second or come third. It was too close to call.

"THE OFFICIALS ARE JUST REVIEWING THE PHOTO FINISH. JUST HOLD ON FOLKS . . . "

Chad and I lay panting in our kayak. We were unable to sit up or take another stroke. We had given all we had.

"AND IT LOOKS LIKE . . . YES . . . THE BOAT FROM BC HAS WON!"

With his chest still heaving, Chad reached back and we pounded fists. "We did it partner," he said.

A large group of teammates were waiting for us back at the dock. "Here they come!"

Coach Cooper steadied our kayak. I had never seen him with such a wide smile. "You guys did it!" he croaked. "I was shouting so much, I lost my voice."

Reaching down, Coach helped us out of our boat. "You made the Club proud, boys." Chad and I followed Coach toward the bleachers where the ceremonies were held. "Now you get to do what I never got to do at the Olympics."

I couldn't imagine anything bigger than making it to the Olympics. "What's that, Coach?"

"Stand on top of the podium." Coach nodded at the platform where the medals would be given out.

The announcer boomed, "FIRST PLACE AND GOLD MEDAL WINNERS IN THE U15, THOUSAND-METRE RACE IS THE TEAM FROM BRITISH COLUMBIA: CHAD BARNES AND FINN HUNTER."

We climbed the three steps. From the top, I could see the whole crowd. Hundreds of people were cheering. Mom and Dad stood right in the middle, clapping and smiling. They'd soon be going their separate ways, but today they were side by side. They were together for me.

Chad and I bent our heads forward to receive our medals from Canada's Olympic champion kayaker. Adam van Koeverden draped a gold medal around each of our necks.

I didn't think I'd ever take it off.

21 Blue SKIES

"Fasten your seat belts," the captain announced. "We'll be landing at Kelowna International Airport in just a few minutes."

I elbowed Chad, who was sitting in the seat next to me. We peered out the window.

"Looks like it's clearing up." I pointed at the sky below, which was more blue than grey.

Chad chuckled. "I hope I never have to paddle through wildfire smoke again. When we rescued Sanjay, my lungs hurt every time I breathed."

I reached out and knuckled bumped him. "That makes two of us."

Far below, there was a thin layer of mist drifting over the Okanagan valley. There were still some wildfires burning far to the north. But as the end of the summer neared, the flames were starting to go out. The smoke was starting to disappear. The skies were starting to clear.

I smiled to myself. Things were looking brighter at home too.

Peering over the top of the seat, I saw Dad sitting a few rows ahead watching a movie. He was chuckling. I thought there would be more laughs in the future, now that we were getting along better. He promised that when we got home, we'd do more things together, like camping, the way we used to. We'd just have to find a new campground after the Glassy Lake wildfire.

I didn't know how he and Ms. Putnam were getting along. It's not like I ever wanted to bring it up. It was too weird to talk about. The only good thing was that I would be moving up to grade nine in a few weeks. She wouldn't be my teacher next school year.

I thought about Madison. She didn't have it so easy, either. I wondered how she was getting along with her mom. I hoped she was able to save enough money to go away for her diving competition.

Chad and I carried our backpacks off the plane. We followed the other passengers walking down the long hall to the terminal. There were only a few paddlers on the plane. Coach Cooper and most of the other team members were still in Ottawa. They hadn't raced yet.

Chad turned to me and smiled. "We did it, partner. But I still feel kind of bad about one thing."

"What's that?" I asked. Why wouldn't he be happy after the best kayaking day of our lives?

"I feel bad for Sanjay," Chad said.

Chad was right. Sanjay was his usual partner. The two of them had worked hard all summer to train for the nationals. He was all set to go to Ottawa. It was just bad luck that a log was floating in the water and he got hurt. "Yeah, I hope Sanjay's arm is getting better," I said. "I feel bad for Niko as well. We tried our best in that race at camp, but I was just too tired. I let him down."

"I think Niko will forgive you," Chad said. "It's hard to let someone down when you try your best."

"I hope so." I nodded.

Chad looked up and saw his dad walking ahead of us. "Hey, Dad, wait up!" Chad flicked his hair and cracked a grin. "See you at the club, partner." Then he ran to meet his father.

I heard footsteps behind me. "I'm glad I caught up to you, Finn," my dad said, wheeling his suitcase.

We walked together toward the gate. "Just a bit farther." I pointed at the sliding doors that opened to the arrivals area.

Dad held up his phone. "I just got a text from Tracy, I mean, Ms. Putnam." His voice was excited.

I knew Dad had been sad not seeing her. He seemed happy to hear from her. "What did she say?"

"That she'd been thinking about things a lot and wanted to talk to me. She sounded friendly."

"So you might talk to her later tonight?" I asked.

Dad shook his head and grinned. "No, I'm going to

talk to her right now. She's waiting for us outside."

We walked through the sliding doors. Sure enough, my teacher was standing there waiting for us. And she wasn't alone. Madison was with her. My eyebrows shot up.

Ms. Putnam smiled and waved. "Here comes our champion!"

We joined my teacher and her daughter. Ms. Putnam gave my dad a hug to welcome him. Dad smiled from ear to ear. It looked like they were back together.

Madison was staring at me. "What's that around your neck, Finn?" she asked.

"Oh, this old thing?" I proudly held the shiny medal out from my chest. "It's nothing really. Just a gold medal for being part of the best U15 kayaking team in the country, that's all." I couldn't help but grin after saying all that.

"I've never gotten a medal from diving," Madison said, reaching out to touch the gold medal.

"I'm sure you will." I nodded.

"I don't know," Madison said. "Paddling seems a lot harder than diving. I don't think I could ever learn."

"I'm pretty sure you could." My grin got somehow bigger. "All you need is a good teacher."

Madison smiled back. But she wasn't smiling at me. She had spotted my teammate with all the hair. "Maybe Chad could teach me."

"I'm sure he'd like that," I laughed.

I was so busy talking to Madison, I didn't see who had snuck up behind me.

"We couldn't wait to see you guys!" Sanjay called out. He was beaming, even though his arm was in a sling. "We saw the results online. We knew you guys could do it."

"You had the best training partners, after all," Niko joked.

"We sure did." I took off my gold medal and hung it around Niko's neck. "You deserve a part of this, partner. I wouldn't be half the paddler I am without you. You pushed me all year to try my best. I owe you, man."

Niko's face lit up as he looked down at the gold medal.

Sanjay's eyes flashed across the airport terminal and he waved. "There's Chad! Let's go talk to him before he goes."

"I'm right behind you," Niko said, running after him.

Ms. Putnam pulled car keys out of her purse and jingled them. "Who needs a ride?" she asked. "I've got plenty of room."

"It will be good to get home," Dad said. "I bet the lawn needs mowing."

I nodded. "I'll be glad to cut it as soon as we get back."

Madison looked at me and frowned.

"But I have a better idea." I smiled back at her.

"Why don't Madison and I split cutting the grass from week to week?"

"That's more like it." Madison grinned.

I still wasn't sure I wanted Madison as a sister. But being friends was just fine with me.